Tales of IRISH Enchantment

MERCIER PRESS

IRISH PUBLISHER – IRISH STORY

PATRICIA LYNCH

Tales of
IRISH
Enchantment

ILLUSTRATED BY SARA BAKER

MERCIER PRESS

Cork

www.mercierpress.ie

Text © Patricia Lynch
Illustrations © Sara Baker, 2010
Foreword © Robert Dunbar, 2010

ISBN: 978 1 85635 681 7

10 9 8 7 6 5 4 3 2 1

A CIP record for this title is available from the British Library

Printed and bound in the EU.

Sara would like to dedicate her work
in this book to

Pal

&

Mike Graham-Cameron

Contents

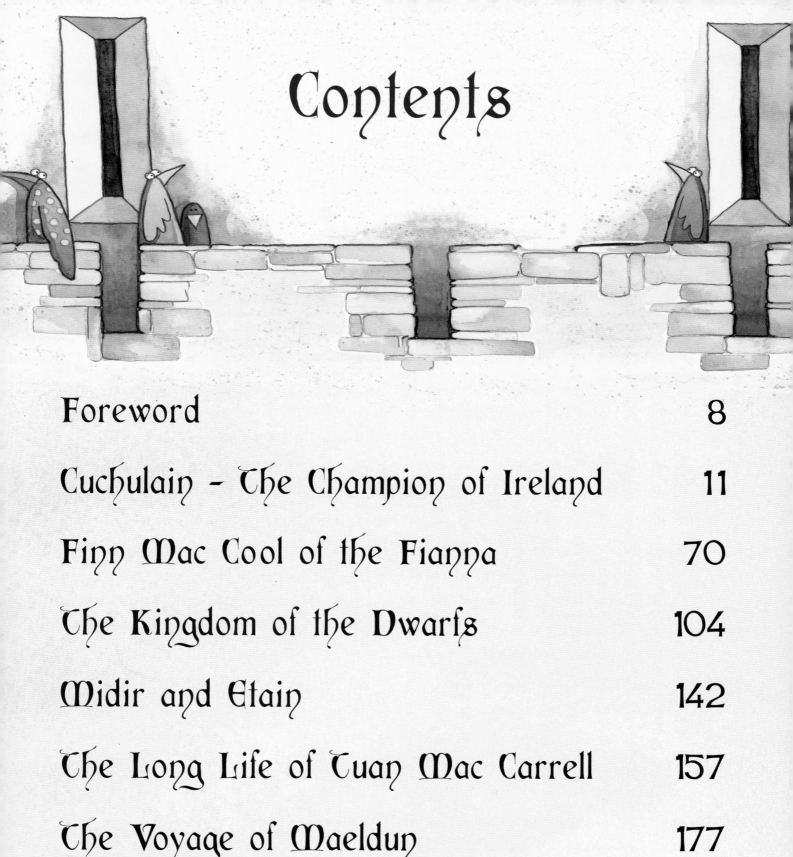

Foreword

'Imagination means looking deeper and seeing beyond the veil'. The words are Patricia Lynch's, first published in 1958 in an article entitled 'There Is a Place for Fantasy', and it would be difficult to find a sentence which better encapsulates the world which, in her children's novels and numerous short stories, she created during her writing lifetime.

Born in Cork in 1898 and brought up in an environment which fostered a love of Irish lore, legend and storytelling, Patricia Lynch's early years saw her lead an essentially nomadic existence, taking her to Britain, Europe and Egypt, before she settled in her late teens and early twenties in London. Here she worked as a freelance contributor to various newspapers and magazines, her writing including the pamphlet *Rebel Ireland*, which was to become a famous eye-witness account of the Easter 1916 events in Dublin, the city that became her permanent home following her marriage in 1922 to the English writer R.M. Fox. By the early 1930s her first children's stories were appearing in serialised form in such newspapers as *The Irish Press*. The novel which subsequently appeared in 1934 as *The Turf-Cutter's Donkey*, and which remains her best known work, had its origins here. Between then and her death in 1972, she had written some fifty children's books and around two hundred short stories.

Although her children's fiction ranges over various genres, covering, among others, fantasy, realism and historical fiction, it is suffused throughout in an atmosphere which portrays Ireland as a place – to quote a phrase from her 1941 novel *Fiddler's Quest* – 'of strange happenings and enchantments'. Her re-tellings of some of the country's oldest stories, such as those in the present collection, first published in 1952, are eloquent testimonies to these 'strange happenings and enchantments' and their lasting appeal. The country itself may have changed almost beyond recognition and the development of Irish children's literature over the past few decades may have taken its young readers into unexpected and increasingly exciting domains, but the human need for magic, for miracle, for 'enchantment' remains – perhaps more than ever – and Patricia Lynch's stories provide all three in abundance.

Robert Dunbar

Children's Books Ireland

Cuchulain The Champion of Ireland

The Finding of Setanta

One summer day, Dectera, a maiden at the court of Conor Mac Nessa, was playing handball with fifty other girls in the meadow before the Grianan, or women's sun house, when suddenly they all vanished. But fifty-one green and gold butterflies fluttered over the grass and flew off among the trees.

Dectera's mother Maga, her father Cathbad the Druid, warriors, women of the court and servants searched for the missing girls. They searched all night and the next day, but found no trace of them. If Dectera alone had disappeared they would have thought her lost, for she was dreamy and always wandering. But surely fifty-one girls could not go astray without someone seeing or hearing them. Yet they had passed along no roads, not a traveller had set eyes on them; hounds trained in the chase could not pick up their tracks.

'They must be under a spell!' declared Cathbad.

Maga went on looking for her daughter. Three years went by and everyone, except her parents, had forgotten Dectera, when one spring morning a flock

of birds alighted on the plain around Emain Macha and began to eat the crops. Another flock invaded the orchards until it seemed not an apple would be left on the trees.

Hearing the shouts of the men who were trying to drive away the birds, the king came out from the palace with Fergus Mac Roy and several other nobles. They attacked the thieves with slings. The birds flew a little way, came down again, waited until the hunters drew near and then rose in the air once more. All day King Conor and his companions tried to catch up with the birds but could not. Without knowing it they were being brought to the fairy rath of Angus, close by the River Boyne.

When it was too dark to go on, or to find their way back, they searched for shelter but all they could discover was a ruined hut on the river bank.

Conor and a few others wrapped themselves in their cloaks and lay down to sleep. The rest had to make themselves as comfortable as they could on the grass outside. Fergus Mac Roy chose the shelter of a low-growing elder bush. But the leaves were still small and the moonlight shone through the twigs onto his face. He could not sleep. He was too restless to lie still, so he went off quietly and strolled beside the Boyne.

He followed a broad, grassy path wondering where it led, when suddenly he saw before him a beautiful building blazing with the light of fires and torches, the gates wide open and the great bronze doors at the top of a flight of wide marble steps were open too.

So surprised he did not think of his crumpled tunic and muddy sandals, Fergus strode up the steps and entered the hall.

A young man, taller even than Conor Mac Nessa, for he was Lugh of the Long Arm, was standing in the hall. With him was the lost Dectera and coming through another doorway were the fifty girls who had disappeared with her.

They crowded round Fergus, making him welcome, asking for news from Emain Macha and telling their adventures; of how they had been enticed into the Land of Youth, how happy they were, so happy they would not come back.

In the morning he returned to the hut by the river, but before he reached it, a baby boy was found sleeping there among the warriors. Dectera had lured them to Lugh's fairy palace so that her son might be taken to Conor Mac Nessa's court and brought up among her own people.

When the king and Fergus Mac Roy returned and the baby with them, the child was given to Dectera's sister. She took care of him with her own son and he was named Setanta.

The Smith's Feast

When Setanta grew old enough he was sent to the court at Emain Macha where he became one of the Troop of Boys who were trained to be warriors.

There were 150, all sons of chieftains and princes. Soon he became their leader for, from the beginning, Setanta was strong and brave. When King Conor and his nobles were invited to a feast at the fort of Cullen, Setanta was chosen to go with them.

Cullen was a smith, but a smith who made swords and spears for the great warriors. His work was famed throughout Ireland, and, because of his skill and wealth it was indeed an honour for a boy to be invited to his home. Setanta was delighted. But when the king and his party were starting, the boys were playing hurley. Setanta would never leave a game half finished and played on.

At last the game was ended and Setanta, without resting, went after the chariots. The marks of the wheels and hoofs were clear in the dust of the road so he had no fear of losing his way.

Tossing his ball of crimson leather stuffed tightly with wool, striking it with his caman before it reached the ground, Setanta ran swiftly hoping to hear the chariots. But he was tired when he started. Soon he stopped tossing the ball and no longer ran. The only sounds were the cool evening wind in the trees, the chatter of birds and the splashing of water from rock to rock.

'Who would have thought they'd be so far ahead?' he thought. 'But I had to play the game out.'

The road dwindled to a path as it entered the forest. The treetops were still tipped with light, but among the trees Setanta moved in shadow. His eyes were keen and he could see the track lying white before him.

Branches rubbed and creaked, there was a continual crackling of twigs and, among the undergrowth, savage calls and terrifying snarls.

'Maybe I should have gone with the chariots,' thought Setanta. 'But how could I, not knowing who had won?'

He moved carefully and, as he glanced over his right shoulder, flaming eyes glared at him between two tree trunks. He stared back in terror. Suddenly the eyes were no longer there and he hurried on.

He heard the patter of feet on the path behind him and tried to run. But he was too weary and instead he forced himself to look back. The moon was rising and a shaft of light pierced the trees. The wind was blowing a scatter of leaves along the path. They danced a little way, then piled up quivering. Farther on other leaves swirled in a circle.

'Aren't I very foolish to be afraid of dried leaves!' Setanta murmured.

The forest was thinning, for the path crossed the narrow end. The boy listened to the tap-tap of his soft leather boots and the sound was like a companion.

He came out from the trees. Bushes grew up from a sea of grass and Setanta went by a wild heath silvered with moonlight. The scufflings of little animals, sleepy complaints from overcrowded nests and the trickling of hidden streams were all about him.

Setanta had never been to Cullen's fort before and he watched anxiously for a light or the sound of voices. He was sure he had come the right way and he had heard the smith lived barely two spear throws beyond the forest.

The ground was rising. He paused as a howl came on the wind.

Was it a wolf? Even a solitary warrior might fear a wolf and Setanta had no arms, only his hurley stick.

The howl came again.

'That's no wolf, but a dog!' decided the boy. 'Cullen's watch dog. I must be nearly there.'

The path topped the crest and once more widened to a road.

On the next ridge Setanta saw a red glow against the darkened sky. He had reached the fort of Cullen.

The Hound of Cullen

Like most of the forts of that day, Cullen's home was surrounded by a bank of beaten earth with a stone wall set on top. A wide wooden gate, closed at sunset and opened at daybreak, was the only entrance. Inside, around the one-storeyed buildings, was space for all the cattle which were driven in each night. Most forts were guarded by armed men. Cullen kept no men at his gate. The only guard was an enormous Irish wolfhound. 'With him at my gate,' boasted the smith, 'I fear nothing but an army.'

Setanta's feet were aching as he climbed the hill. He

could hear music and laughing shouts from the banquet hall and longed to be there. He reached the huge closed gates, but no voice challenged him.

Was the guard sleeping?

Setanta was shivering in the cold night air. His last meal was so many hours back he could not remember what he had eaten. He lifted his caman to beat on the gate and opened his mouth to shout when he heard growling and snuffling so close he leaped away. Something was moving inside the wall. Cullen kept no guard at his gate – only his wolfhound!

Setanta had heard and forgotten.

'No hound shall keep me outside till morning!' he declared and, gripping his caman in his teeth, he leaped at the gate, caught the top by the tips of his fingers, hauled himself up and crouched there.

In the moonlight he saw a great beast gazing at him, eyes gleaming, fangs showing. A queer whimper came from its jaws, then a howl of anger. Springing, it reached for the boy with its powerful claws.

As the hound sprang up, Setanta jumped down. He thrust at it with the curved stick, which was broken in two with one snap of the sharp teeth. Head outstretched it rushed at the boy. Setanta dodged, flung out his hands and caught the brute by the throat. As they wrestled, the hound snarling, Setanta panting, the doors of the hall were flung open and men carrying torches swarmed out, the king and his companions with them.

Through the crowd burst a tall, broad man – Cullen, the smith.

'Let go!' he shouted. 'Let go!' and rushed to save the stranger.

With a last effort Setanta gripped the hound by its forelegs, raised it above his head and flung it crashing to the ground. He heard a muffled growl, then the great head fell sideways. Placing his foot upon the lifeless body, Setanta turned and faced them all.

'By my sword!' cried King Conor. 'I am proud to have this lad in my corps. The size of him and of that huge hound!'

Setanta listened to the praise with sparkling eyes until he noticed the smith standing silently with bent head. Then he understood what he had done. He touched Cullen's hand.

'I killed the hound to save my own life. But I should have stayed outside,' he said. 'I had no right to enter.'

'He was my friend,' sighed the smith. 'He died for the safe-keeping of this dun and he will never guard it again.'

Now there were tears of shame in Setanta's eyes.

'If I could give back the life I have taken, I would,' he told Cullen. 'But give me a pup of this hound and I'll train him to be the equal of his sire. Until then I'll be your hound and I'll guard this fort!'

And from that day Setanta was known as Cuchulain – the Hound of Cullen.

The Promise of Emer

One day Cuchulain heard Cathbad, the Druid, saying that the youth who was given the weapons of a man before nightfall would become one of the most famous warriors in Ireland, but his life would be short and dangerous.

Young Cuchulain went straight before the king and demanded the arms of manhood. Conor smiled, for Cuchulain was small and slight, but handed the boy two full-sized spears. Cuchulain snapped the hafts in pieces between his fingers. Two stronger spears were brought, but he broke them in the same way and went on destroying weapons until Conor sent for a sword and spear of his own. These Cuchulain could not break.

With the weapons the king gave him a war chariot and told him to choose horses from the royal stables.

At this time Emer, daughter of Forgall, Lord of Lusca, was the most beautiful girl in Ireland. Cuchulain loved her the moment he set eyes on her at the court and now that he had a warrior's weapons and chariot he thought he had every right to ask her to marry him.

He set off in his new chariot with Laeg, his friend and charioteer, to Dun Forgall, where the village of Lusk now stands. Cuchulain was proud as they drew up at the gate. Forgall was away so it was Emer who welcomed them.

Cuchulain was quick and dark, gentle and well taught. His crimson cloak with its many-coloured edging was fastened with a brooch of gold and the shield on his back was crimson too with a rim of beaten gold. He laid down his weapons and at once asked Emer to

marry him. She liked him better than any of the young men in her father's dun, but she shook her head.

'It is lucky my father is not here,' she said. 'He would tell you I must marry a man of his choice. And he hasn't chosen you. He intends me to marry a king. But if you were a hero, Cuchulain, a champion of Ireland, then I would choose you. That I promise!'

Cuchulain picked up his sword and spear.

'When I come again, Emer,' he replied, 'I will be the proudest champion in Ireland!'

Away he drove with his red-haired charioteer Laeg and back to Emain Macha, to begin his training as a champion.

In those days champions were trained by women warriors and as the most famous of these was Scatha of the Land of Shadows, Cuchulain went in search of her.

Everyone had heard of her, but no one could tell him where she lived. He travelled through Ireland, through forests and over bogs. At every dun, at every fort he asked for news of Scatha. Not until he reached the northernmost point did he meet one who could show him the way.

An old man, too feeble to fish or hunt, sat in the sun against a rock above the sea and pointed a trembling finger to where Alba lay across the waves.

'Take my boat. I am too old to use it now. It lies on the sand at the foot of this rock. Go straight over. Then keep north. You will come to dark forests, you will pass over desolate moors. There are swift rivers you must ford. There will be rain and cold and mist, always mist. You will come where sea and land are so mingled you would need the wings of a bird to go safely. Then an island of cliffs will loom dimly from the waves and that will be the land you are seeking – the Land of Shadows. I have known many who came this way asking for Scatha. Maybe they found her. They did not return. May you be more fortunate, noble youth.'

The old man's boat was a skin curragh so light it slid over the waves without taking in a drop of water. Cuchulain, brave on land, shuddered when the curragh balanced for an instant on the crest of a wave, then swept into a green hollow, only to be tossed so high it seemed he could touch the clouds.

When he reached the Alban shore he could scarcely walk. But, too impatient to rest, he turned north in search of Scatha.

The Training of a Champion

This was wilder country than Cuchulain had seen before. Rocks piled on rocks; cliffs, precipices with waterfalls; surging streams and sudden lakes: all so savage he thought the forests a protection until he heard the wolves. The inhabitants he encountered, though wild and sullen, were hospitable. There were others, never seen, who shot arrows at him if he stopped to make sure of his path, flung spears as he crept along narrow shelves and hurled rocks to cast him from his scanty foothold.

He was forced to make long journeys inland to cross rivers or arms of the sea which stretched for miles into the mountains. When he asked for Scatha or the Land of Shadows, the people shook their heads and looked at him in wonder. A few advised him to turn back. His boots were in holes, his tunic in rags, but he persevered until he came to the Plain of Ill-luck. Then indeed he was discouraged.

The great bog stretched before him. He could not see the slightest trace of a path and pools of dark water surrounded any rock that rose from the desolation. There were neither flowers, nor grass and no birds sang there.

'Have I been foolish to dream of finding Scatha when only one old man could tell me of her?' he thought. 'Should I turn back while I can?'

As he stood lonely and hesitating, across the quaking bog, treading lightly and surely, came a young man with shining hair and sparkling eyes, whose friendly smile made Cuchulain forget his doubts.

Under his arm he carried a flaming wheel.

'Take this,' he said, 'and do not fear to follow it. When you come to the Perilous Glen this apple will show you the safe way.' He put the wheel into Cuchulain's left hand and a golden apple into the right, then sped off as if his feet were winged.

Cuchulain stared after him until he was only a gleaming blur in the distance.

'Can he be Lugh of the Long Arm?' wondered Cuchulain. 'But why should an Immortal help me?'

He did not know that Lugh was really his father.

His courage returned as he set the wheel rolling over the quaking mud. It blazed with light and the heat from it made a firm path on which Cuchulain walked securely.

As he reached the other side, the flaming wheel rolled out of sight and the wanderer stood gazing into a dark, wooded glen from which rose the howls and snarls of savage beasts.

There was no way round so Cuchulain tossed the golden apple before him. It landed on a high narrow ridge of rock and, springing down on it, he stepped carefully, trying not to hear the appalling sounds coming

up from the depths of the Perilous Glen.

The ridge widened as it climbed above the trees and led Cuchulain to an open meadow.

After the lonely days since he had left Ireland, Cuchulain was thrilled to see a group of lads and young men playing hurley. They dropped their sticks and crowded round him.

Cuchulain discovered that they had come to learn the arts of war from Scatha and that several were from Ireland. One, Ferdia, son of the Firbolg Daman, became his friend and while they were training to be champions they were never parted.

But Cuchulain could not believe he had really arrived at the end of his search.

'Where is Scatha's dun?' he asked. 'I heard she lived on an island called the Land of Shadows.'

Ferdia pointed.

'There is the Land of Shadows and yonder is the dun of Scatha.'

Beyond the sunny meadow the land rose in rock terraces which ended in a cliff. Far below the sea surged in a long winding channel. A swirling mist hung over it and on the other side an island of grey, dripping rocks towered to the sky. As Cuchulain gazed he made out the dun perched far up, a grim terrifying dwelling. He could see it but faintly, for it was shrouded in mist and shadows.

'How can I reach it?' asked Cuchulain.

'You must wait!' Ferdia told him. 'This is our training ground. There is our hall. Tomorrow you will meet Scatha here and she will test you. She does not train all who come to her.'

'I have journeyed so far,' protested Cuchulain. 'Is there no way of coming to her?'

'Look!' said Ferdia. 'There is the Bridge of Leaps and only Scatha can cross it, for the two last feats she teaches her chosen champions are the leap across the bridge and the thrust of the Gae Bolg.'

Cuchulain saw what seemed to be a thin curved plank suspended from cliff to cliff.

'If you step upon one end of that bridge the middle rises and flings you back,' explained Ferdia. 'And if you jump it's so slippery you'll miss your footing and fall into the gulf where the sea monsters are lurking.'

'The bridge is there to be crossed. I will cross it!' declared Cuchulain.

Ferdia persuaded him to bathe and rest at the hall. He was given new boots and fresh clothing, and sat with the others at their evening meal.

The road to the bridge was steep and winding. Cuchulain had forgotten his weariness and while his companions still lingered at the table he started alone.

When he reached the top he looked down and Ferdia raised his hand.

Cuchulain ran at the bridge and, with a flying leap, tried to land upon the middle. It lifted under him and he was tossed back. He could hear shouts from the meadow, some encouraging, some jeering, and tried again.

The fourth time he landed in the centre of the bridge, sprang forward and stood on the Island of Shadows.

He strode on until he reached the dun and there was Scatha in the entrance coming to meet him.

She was so tall Cuchulain did not reach to her shoulder. Her black hair was bound about her head like a shining helmet and her grey eyes stabbed Cuchulain's as if they were twin blades of steel.

She had watched from the dun and was so pleased with Cuchulain's strength and perseverance that she made him her pupil without further test.

Cuchulain stayed with her for a year and a day learning all she could teach him. Often she boasted of his skill for, except Ferdia, she had never known a young man so easy to teach and so eager for all the knowledge she could give.

They fought with her in the wars among the tribes and several times the three of them turned defeat into victory. Scatha felt sad when the time came for them to go back to their own country.

On the last day she taught Cuchulain the use of the Gae Bolg or body spear and gave her own to him for he was the first untried champion she thought worthy to use it. This terrible spear was thrown with the foot and if it entered a warrior's body it filled every limb with its barbs.

Cuchulain said farewell and, at the last moment, he and Ferdia renewed their vows of friendship and promised to help one another as long as they lived.

Champion of Ireland

The evening following his return Cuchulain wandered along the shore of the Grey Lake thinking of his training with Scatha, his friendship with Ferdia and the promise Emer had made before he went away.

He stopped to watch a faint mist which rose from the centre of the lake and turned into a shimmering cloud. Slowly it drifted to the marshy bank, growing denser until a great grey stallion, so perfect Cuchulain gasped in joy, stepped daintily to the path.

Suddenly Cuchulain sprang on the horse's back and gripping its body with his knees, twisted his hands in the thick flowing mane. Rearing it tried to throw him, but Cuchulain clung on. It raced round and round the lake, rising on its hind legs, then flinging down on its head only to jump with all four feet into the air in an effort to toss its rider. Both were covered with foam and sweat, and Cuchulain felt he could hold on no longer when the stallion dropped to a gentle canter and whinnied in submission. From the glen before them came an answering whinny; a coal black steed galloped up and trotted beside the grey.

Cuchulain brought them home and Laeg, his charioteer, harnessed them to the war chariot. Laeg was the finest charioteer in the country; the Grey of Macha, and the Black Steed of the Glen were the best horses and the three of them stayed with Cuchulain to the last day of his life.

Back in his home at Dun Dalgan, now Dundalk, Cuchulain drove in his chariot with the new horses to the highest of the Mountains of Mourne and looked over the land of Ulster. He turned south and gazed across the Plain of Bregia where Tara and Teltin, and Brugh na Boyna lay. Laeg told him the names of all the hills and duns they could see and many beyond their sight.

'Over yonder is the great dun of the sons of Nechtan,' said Laeg.

'Are they the sons of Nechtan who are said to have killed more Ulstermen than are now living on the earth?' asked Cuchulain.

'I have heard that said,' replied Laeg.

'Then drive to the dun of the sons of Nechtan!' ordered Cuchulain.

So they drove to the fort. Before the gate they found a pillar stone and round it a collar of bronze ornamented with writing in Ogham signs:

ANY MAN OF AGE TO BEAR ARMS WHO
READS THIS STONE SHALL HOLD HIMSELF
UNDER GEIS (IN HONOUR BOUND) NOT
TO DEPART WITHOUT CHALLENGING ONE
OF THE DWELLERS OF THIS DUN TO
SINGLE COMBAT.

Cuchulain put his arms about the stone. Pushing and heaving he tugged it out of the earth and flung it into the river below.

'You must be looking for a violent death!' exclaimed Laeg.

Foill, son of Nechtan, hearing the crash and the splashing, came out from the gate of the dun. When he saw Cuchulain he thought he was only a boy and threatened him with his fists.

Cuchulain called to him to bring his weapons for he would not slay an unarmed man.

'You can't kill Foill!' declared Laeg. 'He is protected by magic against the point or edge of any blade.'

'I'm glad you told me that,' said Cuchulain as Foill came out from the dun once more, armed, but without a shield, for he did not think he needed one. He could not take Cuchulain seriously as a fighter.

As Foill rushed upon him with his great sword uplifted, Cuchulain put a ball of iron in his sling and hurled it at the warrior so that it went right through his head. So fierce was his rush that Foill still came on and Cuchulain

had to spring aside while the body of his enemy went on and crashed down the bank into the river.

The other sons of Nechtan came hurrying out. Cuchulain fought and killed them one by one. Ordering everyone out of the dun he set it on fire and drove away leaving it blazing behind.

A flock of wild geese flew overhead, keeping up with his horses. Cuchulain brought sixteen of them down alive with his sling and tied them loosely to his chariot so that their fluttering wings excited the horses until they galloped madly across the plain.

A herd of deer broke from cover and raced before them. Even the Grey of Macha and the Black Steed of the Glen could not come up with them. Cuchulain leaped from the chariot and, chasing after the deer on foot, caught two great stags which he harnessed to the chariot with ropes and so arrived in triumph at the banqueting hall of Emain Macha.

About this time there was a chieftain known as Briccriu of the Poisoned Tongue because he made mischief wherever he was. Now he started the warriors arguing as to who was champion of Erin. It was decided that the three bravest were: Laery the Triumphant, Conall the Victorious, Cuchulain. But which of these should be entitled to the Champion's Portion at a feast could not be agreed.

To prevent a deadly quarrel a demon named The Terrible was called from the lake where he dwelt and asked to decide.

He told them that anyone who wished to be known as the Champion of Erin could chop off his head today. But then the would-be champion must lay his own head on the block tomorrow.

The warriors looked at one another in horror. Only Cuchulain was willing to face the test. Drawing his sword he struck off the head of the demon, who jumped up, seized his head and sprang with it into the lake.

The next morning, the demon, his head back on his shoulders, appeared among them. Cuchulain trembled, yet he kept his promise and laid his head on the block. The demon swung his axe – once, twice, three times – then struck the block with the back of the axe and cried: 'Arise, Cuchulain, Champion of Ireland!'

Now Cuchulain felt he could go to Emer and ask her to keep her promise. He knew her father Forgall the Wily was opposed to him. He sent a message warning her to be ready, ordered his war chariot and beneath the shields and weapons concealed rugs and cushions.

Laeg halted the chariot before Forgall's dun and while the guards at the gate challenged them, Cuchulain leaped 'the hero's salmon leap', which Scatha had taught him, over the high ramparts of the dun.

Emer and her foster sisters were ready, wearing their grandest clothes and all their jewels. Protecting them with his shield Cuchulain fought a way to the gate. As the girls climbed into the chariot, Forgall and his sons returned from a foray. Before they realised what had happened, Laeg shouted to his horses and they bounded forward. Forgall followed with all the chariots and horses he possessed. But he had none equal to the Grey of Macha and the Black Steed of the Glen, nor a charioteer the equal of Laeg. So Emer was brought in safety to Emain Macha.

Conor Mac Nessa loved splendour and he had the marriage of Emer and Cuchulain celebrated with such grandeur that even Maeve of Connaught was envious. A banquet was held lasting for days. The doors of the great hall were flung open so that no one who came need go away fasting. There were hurling and wrestling matches, tournaments of all kinds of fighting, displays of strength and skill. There were storytellers and harpers, who never told the same story or played the same tune twice. Even when Emer and Cuchulain drove off to his dun at Dun Dalgan the feasting went on. They looked back and Emer saw the glow of fires flung against the dark sky and heard singing and music. But Cuchulain heard only the clash of arms and the cries of combat.

The Cattle Raid of Cooley or the Tain Bo Cuailgne

Conor Mac Nessa reigned in Ulster, Maeve and Ailell ruled in Connaught. From their palace of Cruachan they could look over the Plain of Mag Ai and the ruins of that great palace are there in Roscommon to this day.

Ailell was a boastful, easy-going man. Maeve was proud – proud of her titles, Queen of Connaught, Maeve of Fal; proud of her father, the Ard Righ (High King) living at Tara; proud of her wealth and power.

Ailell bragged of his fighting men.

'I have 3,000 well-trained, well-armed young men to protect me. Not a noisy rabble!' declared Maeve.

'I have more horses, serving men and maids than anyone in Ireland, even yourself!' Ailell taunted her.

All night they sat, matching their chariots and horses, the shields and weapons of their warriors, the number of their servants, their clothes and jewels, their flocks of sheep and herds of swine, even the cauldrons and spits in their kitchens. They had as much and no more than one another.

Maeve's eyes were closing with sleep when she remembered Finnbenach (the white-horned), her red bull with white horns. Ailell had nothing to compare with it.

In the morning she ordered her steward, Mac Roth, to bring the wonderful bull that she might display it to the king.

Along came the huge beast, tossing its white horns and walking as proudly as Maeve herself.

'Have you a bull to equal mine?' she asked.

'I have not!' replied Ailell. 'But haven't you noticed it is my herd it leads, not yours? Hasn't Mac Roth told you – it will not stay in the herd belonging to a woman, even if she is Maeve of Connaught!'

Maeve was furious. She turned to the steward, her green eyes flashing, her long, pale face flushed with anger.

'Is there such another bull in Ireland?' she demanded.

'There is indeed!' replied Mac Roth. 'The Brown Bull Donn of Cooley, that is owned by Dara, son of Fachtna in Uladh, is the noblest bull in Ireland.'

Then Maeve was no longer troubled that Finnbenach

had deserted her herd. She longed for the Brown Bull of Cooley more than anything else in the world.

'Go to Dara,' she told Mac Roth. 'Tell him Maeve of Connaught asks for the loan of the Brown Bull for one year. I will give back the bull and fifty heifers with him. If Dara will not be parted from his bull and would live here in Connaught, he shall have as much land as ever he possessed in Ulster, a royal chariot and my friendship.'

Dara was delighted with the offer. He had heard of the splendour of Maeve's court and her offer was generous. But her messengers foolishly boasted that if their mistress's wish was not granted, she and Ailell would take the bull by force.

'Let them come if they dare,' cried Dara, and sent back an answer of defiance.

His rath was in Cooley, between Dundalk Bay and lovely Carlingford Lough, on a height near Warrenpoint, just across the Ulster border.

He was a friendly man and though he was sorry to refuse Maeve, his anger had been roused. His friends in Ulster were far better pleased with his refusal than if he had gone into Connaught with the famous Donn. They did not know how determined Maeve was to take it from them.

'If Dara won't lend his bull, there's nothing to be done but raid for it,' she told Ailell and sent heralds throughout Connaught to summon her host.

'This shall be the biggest raid in the history of Connaught!' declared Maeve and went to her chief Druid to ask what would be her fortune in the fight.

'Among those who will stay behind in peace and those who go into the war there is none dearer to us than ourselves,' said Maeve. 'Tell me our fate. Shall we come alive out of this raid?'

'Who comes or comes not back in safety, you shall come,' said the Druid.

As they returned, her charioteer swung the horses to the right so that they should carry the good omen with them. But they were only halfway to Cruachan when, before them, right up against the horses, Maeve saw a young girl with long fair hair, dressed in green, and with a shuttle of gold she wove a web upon a loom.

'Who are you?' cried Maeve, startled by the girl's sudden appearance. 'And what are you weaving?'

'I am the prophetess Fedelma from the Fairy Mound of Croghan,' replied the girl. 'I am weaving the four provinces of Ireland together for the raid.'

'Can you see our host in the battle?' asked Maeve eagerly.

'I see them all red,' replied Fedelma.

'Yet there is not one of the Ultonian warriors can lift a spear against us,' said the queen, 'for the Curse of Macha is upon them.'

'I see your host all red!' repeated the girl. 'I see one man against them

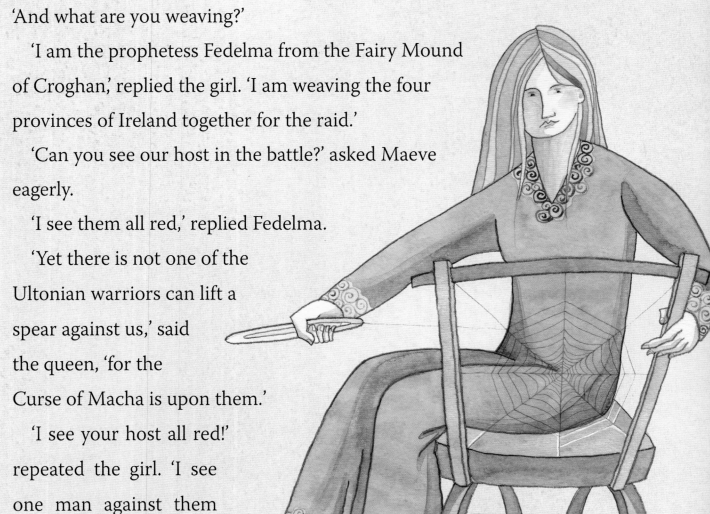

– slender, young, gentle, but in battle a hero and his name is Cuchulain!'

Fedelma vanished and Maeve drove on to Cruachan wondering.

Long ago, because of a great wrong done to her by the warriors of Ulster, Queen Macha had laid a curse upon them that, for generations, in the hour of their greatest peril, they should lie stricken and helpless. This was the Debility of the Ultonians. But because Cuchulain was the son of Lugh, a god, he was not affected.

At dawn the great army started on the march for Ulster. Fergus Mac Roy, who came from the north, led the host and kept a watch for Cuchulain.

All the champion could hope to do was delay the invaders until the Ultonians had recovered. He went into the forest and, standing on one leg, using only one hand and closing one eye, he cut an oak sapling and twisted it into a circle. On this he cut in Ogham letters how the circlet was made and put the host of Maeve under **geis** not to pass by for twelve hours unless one of them had, in the same way, made a similar circlet.

He put the circlet round the pillar stone of Ardcullin and went back to the mountains.

When Maeve and her army came to Ardcullin, they found the circlet and its message. They knew they must do the champion's bidding or great evil would come upon them. There wasn't one of them could imitate Cuchulain's feat, so they camped there for the night. A heavy snowstorm swept over them, their tents and cooking pots were far behind and they spent many wretched hours. But in the morning they marched over the whitened plain into Ulster.

Cuchulain kept ahead and hiding among the rocks, saw two chariots sent on by Maeve to give warning of any unexpected enemy. As he came out the warriors rushed at him with uplifted swords but he killed them both and their drivers too.

With one stroke of his sword he cut down a forked tree and drove it deep into the ford, now called Athgowla or the Ford of the Forked Pole, where Maeve must pass. On each prong he placed a head. The army came marching along, but halted when they saw this terrible sight. The tree with its gory burden blocked the ford and no chariot could pass until it had been taken away.

First one man, then two tugged at the tree. It was planted so deeply they could not move it an inch. A rope was tied about it and fastened to a chariot. Not until late that night and after seventeen chariots had been broken in the struggle, could they tear out the tree!

Next day Cuchulain, still watching, heard the sound of an axe felling trees. Going into the forest he found one of the Connaught men cutting chariot poles of holly.

'We have damaged our chariots in chasing that famous deer, Cuchulain,' he explained. 'My master, Orlam, is proud of his chariots.'

'Shall I help you?' asked Cuchulain.

'If you could trim the poles as I cut them, I'd be thankful,' replied the man.

Taking the long straight branches at the top, Cuchulain drew them against the set of twigs through his toes, then ran his fingers down them.

'There you are!' he said.

The man stared at the poles, smooth and shining as though they had been planed and polished.

'I've never seen that job done better,' he said. 'Yet I do not think this is your proper work. Who are you?'

'I am Cuchulain!' said the champion.

The Connaught man stared doubtfully. The hero was small and slight. He had chatted and laughed as they worked together. Now he stood straight, his eyes blazed and that hero light which shone about his head in battle quivered like a flame.

The man trembled and dropped his axe.

'Don't be afraid. I never harm messengers, or unarmed men,' Cuchulain told him. 'Run now and tell your master Orlam, that Cuchulain is on his way.'

Forgetting his axe, the man rushed from the forest, but Cuchulain raced him and meeting Orlam first, cut off his head. Maeve saw him a moment as he waved this trophy of war upon the hillside. Then he vanished in the mist. Cuchulain was alone and the great western army seemed very secure in its camp. But he did not leave them in peace for an hour. Across a narrow pass leading to the Plain of the Swineherd, he flung an oak and placed a geis upon it so that until one of the chiefs should leap this in his chariot, the army must not go by.

Thirty made the attempt; thirty horses fell and thirty chariots were smashed before Fergus Mac Roy leaped clear over the oak.

As Maeve sat outside her tent looking on at two men wrestling, a stone from an unseen sling killed a tame bird sitting on her shoulder and as she started in surprise, another struck the pet squirrel from her knee.

Men dared not leave the camp alone. Even when they were in twos and threes, Cuchulain attacked and killed them. Daring young fighters, longing to gain fame, went in search of him and did not return. Camp followers became afraid to seek plunder unless they went in bands of twenty or thirty.

'He has but one body!' cried Maeve indignantly. 'Let but a tried champion go against him!'

She tried to persuade Fergus Mac Roy to challenge Cuchulain. But Fergus would not. He would lead the army of Maeve and Ailell against the Ultonian army. But he would not attack Cuchulain whom he had known as a boy when they were both at Emain Macha.

One moonlit night Cuchulain looked down on the camp from a height and every time a face showed white, he used his sling. Men, half-asleep, heard groans around them but thought they were dreaming. In the morning a hundred warriors lay dead.

Maeve now sent a messenger to Cuchulain offering him wealth and land if he would desert the Ultonians. They were curious to see one another and talked across a deep, narrow stream. Maeve had seen the hero in his battle frenzy, his eyes protruding, his muscles swollen, the red light flaming upward from his head. Now she saw a slim, boyish man, who would not swerve from his allegiance to Ulster if she gave him half of Connaught.

Cuchulain had seen Maeve only from a distance. Now he looked upon her proud beauty, her yellow hair falling like a cloak around her, her green eyes, her pale face. Her rich clothes and wonderful jewels, her splendid chariot with restless, stamping horses, made him realise the grandeur of her court. He knew her courage and that she was the cleverest ruler in Ireland.

'Yet she'd risk everything for the sake of a brown bull!' he thought.

At last Fergus Mac Roy persuaded Cuchulain not to harry Maeve's army if they would send only one warrior at a time against him. While they fought, the army could march. But when one was victorious, they must camp until the next day.

'Better to lose one man each day than a hundred each night,' said Maeve.

The single combats began at the Ford of Dee, now called Ardee.

In his lonely camp Cuchulain practised the feats Scatha had taught him and played chess with Laeg, his charioteer. Day by day young chieftains from Maeve's army came out to challenge him and Cuchulain was always the victor.

Soon it was hard to find warriors worthy to fight the champion and Maeve began to regret the treaty she had made.

She sent back to Connaught for Natchrantal, a chief famous for his size and skill with arms. When he came and saw the Ulster champion he was very scornful.

'He is only a boy and yet you are afraid of him. I thought better of Maeve's warriors!'

He refused to take shield or sword, but carried only a few light spears.

Natchrantal came upon Cuchulain fowling on the lake below his camp and, without warning, cast one of his spears. Cuchulain jumped to one side and, as the blade struck the ground, took aim with his sling at a waterfowl.

Each time Natchrantal cast a spear Cuchulain sent a shot after a bird. At the seventh cast a flock of birds rose from the water and Cuchulain followed them out of sight.

Back at the royal camp Natchrantal told what had happened.

'I knew it!' cried Maeve. 'He can fight young lads, but he flies from a seasoned warrior.'

'You are wrong!' declared Fergus Mac Roy. 'Cuchulain will not fight any but fully armed men. Let Natchrantal go tomorrow fully armed and he will find Cuchulain ready to meet him.'

When Natchrantal went out the following day, carrying shield and sword and his heavy spears, he found Cuchulain waiting on the mountainside. Yet still he could not believe that this quiet young man was a great champion.

'Are you indeed Cuchulain?' he shouted.

Cuchulain waved his hand.

'You will find the man you seek down yonder glen.'

As Natchrantal strode off, Cuchulain rubbed blackberry juice on his face to pretend he had a beard.

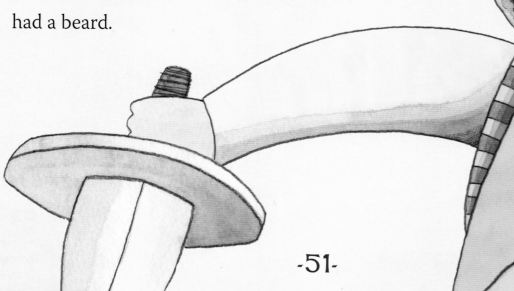

'If fools judge by appearance we must let them have their way,' he said to Laeg, laughing.

And he raced after Natchrantal.

The Connaught man heard the jangle of arms and swung round.

'I heard you were looking for me,' said Cuchulain.

'Are you Cuchulain?' asked Natchrantal.

'I am, and I will give you choice of arms though you are the challenger.'

'I choose spears!' replied Natchrantal, throwing his spear.

As it whistled through the air Cuchulain leaped over it.

'Now do the same with mine!' he said.

He flung his so high even he himself could not have leaped over it, yet so quickly and surely that the spear came straight down upon Natchrantal, piercing his head.

'I am indeed slain by the Champion of Ireland!' he said, as he fell dead.

While they fought, a third of Maeve's army made a sudden march through Ulster, burning and plundering. The Brown Bull had taken refuge with a herd of cows in a glen at Slievegullion in Armagh. The amazed raiders found Donn of Cooley there and drove him off in triumph. Cuchulain watched their return and hurried down to meet them. He attacked and killed the leader, a fair-haired man named Buic, son of Banblai. But the raiders drove the herd on and he could not stop them.

Maeve watched their coming with delight.

'Now I have defeated Cuchulain and the Cattle Raid of Cooley is ended!' she said.

At the Ford

Maeve was wrong. She was satisfied. She had captured the Brown Bull and Ailell could not boast that he held the finest bull in the country, for Finnbenach and Donn of Cooley were equally strong, fearless and handsome. But Maeve had started a war and every day came allies from the south and west, eager for a share of the fighting and plunder, while Cuchulain was still the solitary champion of Ulster.

He sat beside his half-dead fire with his head in his hands, feeling lonely and defeated, and weary of fighting. If only he could have won back the Brown Bull he would have been strong and tireless. Now he wondered how long this terrible, senseless war would last.

A golden light fell across his face and, looking up, he saw coming by Maeve's encampment, the young man who had helped him when he was on the road to Scatha's dwelling. He would have jumped to his feet in respect but a powerful hand pressed him down and he sank back too weary to resist.

'Sleep softly, Cuchulain, and I will watch here with you.'

Then Cuchulain slept and dreamed while a voice sang softly above him:

Sleep hero while the god of light
Watches your foes throughout the night,
And dream of finer battles far
Than this vain Raid of Cooley.

Ferdia shall die; Cuchulain too:
The boys of Ulster fade like dew.
Yet Maeve shall lose, although she wins
This Cattle Raid of Cooley.

The host of Maeve saw on the mountain the golden light which surrounded Lugh and they were afraid.

At Emain Macha the warriors still lay ill and helpless. Only grown men suffered from the Curse and when the boys who were trained there heard of Cuchulain's desperate struggle, they put on their light armour, took their spears and with King Conor's young son, Follaman, leading them, marched southward.

'I will never go home until I carry with me the diadem of Ailell's!' he declared.

Not one of them returned. Three times the 150 young heroes attacked Maeve's army. Three times their own number were killed. But in the end they were overcome.

Cuchulain slept for three days and nights. When he awoke, fresh and ready for battle, he feared the invaders might have passed on without check or challenge.

Lugh told him how the boy corps from Emain Macha had taken his place.

'How many live?' asked Cuchulain quietly.

'Not one!' answered Lugh. 'Conor's son led them. They fought and died like warriors.'

'And I slept while they were fighting for me!' cried the champion. 'But I'll avenge them.'

The battle fury came on him. He leapt into his chariot and, with Laeg beside him, drove the Grey of Macha and the Black Steed of the Glen. Round and round Maeve's camp they thundered, ploughing the earth until it rose into ramparts. The scythes upon the wheels caught the bodies of the crowded host so that they were piled in a wall. Cuchulain shouted and all the demons and goblins in Erin answered back. The army was panic-stricken and men, rushing about in terror, fought one another, while many died from horror and fear.

This was called the Carnage of Murthemney.

Now the Clan Catalin came against Cuchulain. Catalin was a wizard who considered himself and his twenty-seven sons as one person. What one did they all did and their weapons were so poisonous that a man lightly grazed by one would die in nine days. When the clan met Cuchulain each threw a spear. Cuchulain caught the twenty-eight spears on his shield and drew his sword to cut them off. Clan Catalin rushed upon him, flung him down and forced his face into the stony earth.

Fiacha from Ulster, who was with Maeve's host, could not bear this unequal fight. Rushing forward he cut off the twenty-eight hands with one stroke and Cuchulain, staggering to his feet, destroyed the whole clan. So, luckily, there was no one left to tell Maeve what Fiacha had done.

๛

Ferdia, Cuchulain's old comrade, was fighting for Maeve. But though she asked him again and again to challenge Cuchulain, he refused.

She taunted him and threatened that the rhymers would make ballads against him and years after his death they would still be sung.

But if he would go out against the champion, her daughter, the lovely Finnavair, would be his wife, and lands and great wealth would be his.

Then Ferdia went, slowly and unwillingly. He had never forgotten his friendship with Cuchulain. Although he was on the other side he was proud of his friend's great skill and courage, and gloried in his exploits.

'If we had stayed together, not even Maeve and all her army could have beaten us!' he thought.

Ferdia drove to the ford before the sun had risen and while the river was still hidden in mist. He lay in his chariot, dreaming of their early years together and wondering which of them should die, for he was sure that when he and Cuchulain met, only one of them would depart alive.

Not until dawn did he hear the champion's chariot approaching. The two friends looked at one another across the ford.

'I did not expect you, Ferdia, to come to do battle with me,' said Cuchulain. 'When we were with Scatha we shared feast and fight; we shared one bed and where you went, I went with you. In those days I would not have believed that my friend Ferdia would live to challenge me!'

'It must be!' replied Ferdia. 'Forget our old comradeship, Hound of Ulster! My hand is the one that shall wound you. Choose your weapons!'

'You have the first choice!' Cuchulain told him. They began with javelins and they were so well matched that the weapons darted backwards and forwards across the river without once drawing blood.

Cuchulain smiled. But they were warriors and Maeve's army watched from a distance.

When the sun was overhead they began casting their heavy spears and though both were wounded, there was nothing to choose between them. They might have been back with Scatha practising in the Land of Shadows.

Evening came. They flung down their weapons and Cuchulain rushed into the ford to go to Ferdia. But Ferdia met him halfway. They clasped hands, then sat by the same fire, talking of long ago. All that they had of

healing ointment and food and drink they shared, and when they lay down on their beds of green rushes they almost forgot the war which had brought them there.

Next day they continued to fight. All day they thrust and slashed and, when night came, they were so weary and covered with wounds they ceased the combat without a word.

But once more they were friends.

In the morning Cuchulain, aching all over, looked at Ferdia and saw his pale face and dimmed eyes.

'Turn back, Ferdia!' he said. 'Let the fight be over or it will be a fight to the death. Do not give your life for the daughter of Maeve.'

'I cannot turn back!' declared Ferdia. 'I have promised. Take the victory. It will be yours. I do not fear death. But if I went back now my honour would be broken in Rathcroghan. Maeve has been my undoing. Let us begin. What weapons should we use?'

That night they parted in silence and misery. Cuchulain slept with his charioteer on the north side of the river and Ferdia on the south.

When dawn came they put on full battle dress. Each felt this was the last day and they decided to use all their weapons.

They began quietly, but gradually the anger of warfare came upon them. They forgot their friendship and fought savagely as though they had been enemies all their lives.

The sparkling river was red with their blood and splashed over them as they struggled in the centre of the ford. Ferdia gave Cuchulain a blow with his gold-hilted sword that buried it in his body. Cuchulain leaped into the air but Ferdia caught him on his shield and flung him off. From each bank the charioteers shouted warnings and encouragement to their masters. But neither heard.

At last Cuchulain called to Laeg for the Gae Bolg – the body spear – and Ferdia knew the fight was ending. He tried to protect himself with his great shield, but Cuchulain flung the terrible spear high and it pierced Ferdia's chest. He fell backwards and Cuchulain, running to him, lifted his friend and carried him to the north side.

'It is not right that I die by your hand, Hound of Ulster!' said Ferdia, and spoke no more.

Cuchulain fell fainting beside him. Laeg cried out, 'Rise up, Cuchulain! Maeve's army will be on us! There'll be no more single combats now!'

'Why should I rise again?' asked Cuchulain. 'I would sooner lie dead here than my friend Ferdia.'

But Laeg carried him away to Emer at Dun Dalgan. Maeve had the body of Ferdia placed in a grave with a mound over it and a pillar stone with his name and descent carved on it in Ogham.

The Rousing of Ulster

Still the warriors of Ulster lay helpless. Sualtam, Cuchulain's foster father, was no great fighter and dared not stand beside his son in the struggle against the southern army. But when he saw Cuchulain was likely to be defeated, he mounted the Grey of Macha and rode through Ulster, trying to rouse the people.

'The western raiders are upon us!' he shouted. 'Ulster is destroyed. Fight for your homes!'

But he could not stir them to battle.

He came to Emain Macha and there was Conor the King, Cathbad the Druid, chiefs and warriors, recovering from the Debility, yet still only half-awake. Sualtam rode the grey horse in among them.

'Cuchulain holds the Gap alone!' he cried. 'Arise and defend Ulster!'

They listened and nodded but could not move.

Angry and despairing, Sualtam tugged at the reins to turn the horse about. The grey reared, almost unseating him. Sualtam fell sideways upon the sharp rim of his shield, which severed his neck, and the head fell to the ground. Yet still it cried to the king, appealing to him not to abandon Cuchulain. Conor sleepily ordered a servant to place the head upon a pillar. Even then the voice sounded through the palace – 'Rise, King Conor, or your land will be taken from you! Awake, chieftains of Ulster! The invaders are upon us!'

The horse with its headless rider clattered out of the palace and still the head cried its warning.

Slowly the words sent their meaning into Conor's mind. The chieftains stared at one another in amazement and Macha's spell was lifted from them. Conor stood up and they stood with him. Quickly they seized their weapons while the king sent messengers throughout the land calling the men of Ulster together.

Maeve heard the Ultonians were advancing. Standing on the Hill of Slane she saw the Plain of Gorach covered with deer and other wild beasts.

'What brings them here?' she asked.

'They have been driven out of the forest by the Ulstermen,' replied Fergus Mac Roy, who watched beside her.

A mist rolled over the plain. From it came thunder and flashes of light.

'What is this?' asked Maeve.

'The mist is the deep breathing of the warriors as they march,' declared Fergus. 'The light is the flashing of their swords and spears, and the thunder, the tumult of their chariots.'

'We have warriors to meet them!' said Maeve proudly.

'You will need them all!' Fergus Mac Roy told her.

Cuchulain heard the march of the Ultonians too and forgetting his grief over Ferdia's death, joined them in the battle at noon. Before dark the host of Connaught was in flight.

Cuchulain came up with Maeve as she reached the Shannon. She would not fly but halted her horses and waited.

'You are safe from me, Queen of Connaught, now that you are beaten,' he said.

Then, proud though she was, Maeve asked him to stop the slaughter of her retreating men.

'That will I gladly do,' replied Cuchulain.

And until the last of her men had crossed the river Cuchulain stood guard to see they went safely. Then he returned to Ulster and Maeve to Connaught.

The Brown Bull was before her and meeting the White Bull on the Plain of Ai, the two great beasts charged one another. The Brown Bull caught Finnbenach on his horns and flung him to the ground, bellowing and trampling until the White Bull was dead. Then raging from Rathcroghan to Tara, the Donn of Cooley fell dead with exhaustion at the Ridge of the Bull.

After that peace was made between Maeve and Ulster.

The Vengeance of Maeve

In a little while Maeve forgot that but for Cuchulain her whole army would have been destroyed. She blamed him for her defeat in battle and for the death of the two bulls. She did not know which she regretted most – Finnbenach, who refused to stay in her herd, or Donn, who had never been in it.

'There have never before been two such bulls in Ireland,' she said sorrowfully, 'nor ever will again.'

She thought and thought of her loss and her defeat until she determined on revenge.

Cuchulain lived happily with Emer. He had recovered from his wounds and slowly his strength came back. But still he grieved, for Ferdia's death was always at the back of his mind. He knew, too, that Maeve would never forgive him. She was too proud, too warlike, too much a lover of victory.

The wizard Catalin, who had been killed at the ford with his twenty-seven sons, left behind him his wife and six other children, three sons and three daughters. They were ugly, misshapen and loved evil. They were skilled in magic and Maeve gave them leave to do all the harm they could to Cuchulain.

While the children of Catalin prepared charms and spells, Maeve sent secret messages to all the other enemies of the Hound of Ulster. Hearing that the Curse of Macha had fallen again upon the Ultonians she assembled her army and marched north.

Once again Cuchulain came to meet her. But the wizards made him think that wayside bushes and the trees of the forest were armed men. On every side he imagined he saw smoke rising from burning homes. He fought phantoms until his mind was filled with horror. Cathbad the Druid persuaded him to rest in a quiet glen where Niam, wife of his friend Conall of the Victories, took care of him and made him promise not to leave the dun without her knowledge.

Bave, one of the daughters of Catalin, entered the dun in the form of a handmaiden and put a spell on Niam so that she wandered away and was lost in the woods. Bave then returned to the dun as Niam and bade Cuchulain go forth to save Ulster once more.

Cuchulain ordered Laeg to bring out his chariot and harness the horses. The Grey of Macha resisted and when, at last, Laeg forced the yoke upon him, big tears poured down the Grey's face.

Cuchulain came to his own dun at Murthemney and Emer implored him not to be led by phantoms, but he would not listen and said goodbye. His mother, Dectera, was with Emer and she poured him a goblet of wine. As he put it to his lips the wine turned to blood and he flung it down.

'I shall not return from this battle,' he told them as he drove away.

He came to a ford. A girl was kneeling on the river bank, weeping as she washed a heap of bloodstained clothes. She lifted them from the water and Cuchulain saw they were his. But as he crossed the ford she vanished.

When Cuchulain came near Slieve Fuad, south of Armagh, his enemies had gathered to meet him and he drove straight at them. Hurling his spear, he sent it through nine men, killing them all. It was drawn out and flung back, missing Cuchulain, but striking Laeg, his friend and charioteer, who, calling 'Farewell, Hound of Ulster!' dropped on the floor of the chariot and died there.

Now the Grey of Macha was wounded and broke away, followed quickly by the Black. Cuchulain knew that he would never drive them again.

Maeve's warriors came near and Cuchulain looked calmly at them.

'My wounds have made me thirsty,' he said. 'Will you let me drink at the stream?'

They stood out of his way and, walking slowly, he went down to the river. He drank and washed away the blood, then came back to the bank.

A pillar stone stood there. He leaned against it and bound himself to it with his girdle. He took his sword in his right hand and laid his shield on the ground at his feet.

He died there, standing, with his face to his enemies; and the glory of Ulster died with him.

Finn Mac Cool of the Fianna

The Old Men in the Forest

Before the time of Finn Mac Cool, only those who belonged to Clan Bascna or Clan Morna could enter the Fianna and become warriors of the High King, pledged to serve him and to fight invaders.

In a struggle over the leadership, Cool, chief of Clan Bascna, was killed at Knock. He was married to Murna, grand-daughter of Nuada of the Silver Hand. When her husband was killed, she hid in the forest along the slopes of Slieve Bloom and her son was born there. She called him Demna and to keep him safe from Clan Morna, gave him to Bobdall, a druidess, and Luacha, a woman warrior, who lived together.

Demna's hair was so golden and his skin so fair, his name was soon changed to Finn, the fair one. He grew very quickly and before he was six, he went off one day with a sling Luacha had made for him. On a wide pool he saw seven ducks and, casting a stone from his sling, cut off the tail feathers of the largest. This was his first chase and proudly he carried home the feathers.

The two women told him of his father's death and warned him of the

enmity of Clan Morna. Luacha taught him to use a spear and sword, to run swiftly and noiselessly, to aim surely, until she could teach him no more.

She had weapons made for him at a forge in the forest – weapons large enough for a man's use though he was still only a boy.

'Take your weapons and go into the world,' she told him. 'Who wishes to travel far must start early.'

Since he had heard of his father's death Finn had one ambition – to take his place. But he was poor and powerless. Bobdall and Luacha had given him all they had and left themselves the poorer.

Running swiftly as the woman warrior had taught him, he journeyed into Connaught, resting only when he could scarcely put one foot before the other, until he came to the Rath of Lia, Chief of Clan Morna and Treasurer to the Fianna. He had charge of the Treasure Bag, a large pouch made of crane's skin, filled with magic weapons and jewels which had been preserved from the days of the Danaans.

As Lia came out of his gate, a man walking beside him to carry the precious bag, Finn shouted a challenge: 'I am here to kill you, Lia of Clan Morna, as once you killed my father, Cool of the Fianna!'

Lia drew his sword, but Finn pierced him with a single cast of his spear. He snatched the bag from the attendant, who gazed in fear at the fierce, fair-haired youth. Finn sped back to Slieve Bloom country. He travelled during the night and slept all day, for he knew the Fianna would seek him out.

He gave some of the jewels to Bobdall and Luacha, and then looked for the survivors of Clan Bascna. He found them – a few old men, living miserably in the heart of the western forest. They were too weak to build huts or to hunt for food. They lived on wild berries and the bony fish they caught in the forest streams. The only comfort they

had was the fire which they kept burning from one year's end to another.

Finn brought them guards and servants, had a fine house built and furnished for their use. Then he handed them the Treasure Bag.

'Guard this well!' he told them. 'When I return I will be head of the Fianna!'

The Salmon of Wisdom

Finn had learned magic from Bobdall and how to use sword and spear from Luacha. The druidess had once been renowned for her wisdom and the woman warrior for her courage. But of late years they had grown into a pleasant way of living, Bobdall finding happiness in the making of a garden and the curing of sickness, and Luacha in fishing, snaring birds and caring for a child like Finn.

'You'll never become Chief of the Fianna living here with us,' said Bobdall. 'You'll need more wisdom than most men. Danger will make you brave, but wisdom must be learned and there isn't much of that here.'

They often talked of Finegas, an old poet, who lived beside the Boyne River. He was the cleverest man in all Ireland, they said.

'It's true, I'll need knowledge,' decided Finn. 'If I am to be Chief of the Fianna, I must know all there is to know. I wonder would Finegas teach me?'

So he journeyed to the Boyne.

Finegas had built himself a hut. But he spent so much time in learning

and thinking that when the roof leaked he merely moved his seat, resolving to gather saplings and mend his hut when the weather was dry. When the rain ceased, he forgot the leak. By this time one side of the hut was open to the weather and almost all the roof had gone.

Finegas ate only when he was hungry. As he would not spend time on planting, hunting or fishing, he often felt hungry, though the river at his door held many fine fish.

The only fish the poet wanted to catch was the Salmon of Wisdom who often swam by, glistening as he leaped and plunged. But the poet had no rod or line that would hold such a monster. Only for the hazel bushes which overhung the stream and whose nuts dropped into the water, the old man would have starved. The nuts were very large and milky, for they were the Nuts of Knowledge.

The more he ate of them, the wiser Finegas became. But he was tired of nuts when, one morning, Finn appeared before the hut.

Finegas was only just awake. His bed of rushes was old and hard, and his bones ached. He scowled at Finn, then wondered if the boy had come with a present of cakes or honey.

'What do you want?' he asked.

'I have come to learn poetry and wisdom from you,' replied Finn respectfully. 'Bobdall the druidess and her friend Luacha told me you were the cleverest man in all Ireland.'

Finegas sat looking at the lad silently. He liked solitude, yet he was lonely. He dreaded a noisy, troublesome young fellow, who would think he had gained the wisdom of the world before he had discovered his own ignorance. Yet this tall, fair boy pleased him.

Finn seemed to be gazing on the ground at his feet. But he saw the ruined roof and walls, the few poor bits of delph, the uncomfortable bed, the broken stool and, though he still admired the learned man, he was sorry for him.

'I can fish and cook. I can build and plant. I can make sandals and mend tunics,' he said. 'Take me as a pupil, Finegas, and I will be a good servant.'

The old man made up his mind suddenly.

'You have been well trained,' he said. 'Therefore you have the foundations of knowledge. I will be your master. Build up the fire and give me some breakfast.'

Finn had brought a rod and line with him. He sat on his heels at the edge of the bank and, while the poet lay on his back meditating, caught two fine fish. He cleaned them and made a fire. As the fish were grilling on two sharp-pointed, pronged stakes, he mixed a thin, round cake of crushed hazelnuts. As this was baking in the hot ash, he saw a line of wild bees streaming from a hollow tree. When the last one flew away, he plunged in his knife and cut away a section of honey. He rolled a log over to the fire.

'Will you be seated, Master?' he said to the old man.

'I must be wise or how could I have such a pupil!' thought Finegas, feasting as he had not feasted for years.

After breakfast, Finn gathered armfuls of rushes and thatched the roof of the hut, making it so close and firm neither wind nor rain could enter. He cut saplings and strengthened the walls, made a fresh bed for the poet, then commenced to fix a better fireplace just by the entrance.

As he worked he sang:

I who long for wisdom's power,
Learning and the poet's skill,
Clean and cook, and meekly stand,
Waiting on an old man's will.

Much he knows and seeks to know;
But if I had half his art,
I'd not dream beside a pool;
In the world I'd take my part.

Slowly pass the quiet hours;
Slowly drift the days along,
Drift the hazelnuts of knowledge
Out of sight and out of song.

Finegas sat on the bank in the sunshine and fished. His rod was split, his line frayed and he could not catch the smallest trout. Impatiently he flung the rod into the river and, as it floated away, a huge fish raised its head from the water and gaped at the angry poet.

'Fintan!' he cried. 'Fintan – the Salmon of Wisdom! I have lost my chance!'

Finn had been piling small, thick logs by the hearth. He swung round.

'The Salmon of Wisdom!' he exclaimed. 'Where?'

The poet pointed. But Finn saw only a line of foam where an unseen fish swam rapidly away.

'I've heard of the Salmon of Wisdom!' he said slowly.

'Don't mind me!' said Finegas. 'I meant nothing. 'Twas a big fish. That's all!'

He didn't want the boy to know he had been trying to catch Fintan for years, nor to learn that he who ate this salmon would possess the wisdom of ages.

'Don't vex yourself,' Finn told the old man. 'I'll make a rod that will hold the biggest fish that swims the river!'

Next morning when Finegas, lying snug on his thick bed of birch boughs padded with dry moss, opened his eyes, a handsome willow rod with a strong coiled line lay beside him.

He was so eager to go fishing with it he could hardly wait for breakfast. He went a little way from the hut, beyond some tall bushes where Finn couldn't see him and propped his rod against a rock.

Finn was making a comfortable chair to rest his master's frail bones when he heard a shout and rushed to see what was happening. He found Finegas sprawling on his back and a huge silvery fish flapping beside him.

'That's the biggest fish I've seen!' declared Finn. 'Is it a salmon?'

'What other kind of a fish would it be!' replied the poet sharply. 'I'll have salmon for my supper. And, listen now! I want it all! Don't touch a morsel!'

Finn hummed to himself as he cleaned and cooked the salmon.

'There's enough fish for two grown men!' he thought. 'And poor greedy old Finegas wants every bit. He'll not be able to eat that at one meal! Ah, well, it will save me trouble tomorrow. I'll have time to learn some poetry and maybe a bit of wisdom. What with cleaning and mending and cooking, I've learned less since I've been here than ever before.'

Finn turned the salmon, touching it with his fingers. It was so hot they were burned and he put his thumb in his mouth to suck away the pain.

'Oh!' he cried, standing up. 'When did I learn so much!'

'Finn!' called the poet. 'Is the salmon cooked?'

'It is indeed, Master!' Finn called back.

He brought the great fish on a board, for their largest platter wasn't big enough to hold it. He set it down before Finegas and they looked at one another.

'Your face is changed. Your eyes look beyond me. You have eaten the salmon!' said the poet accusingly.

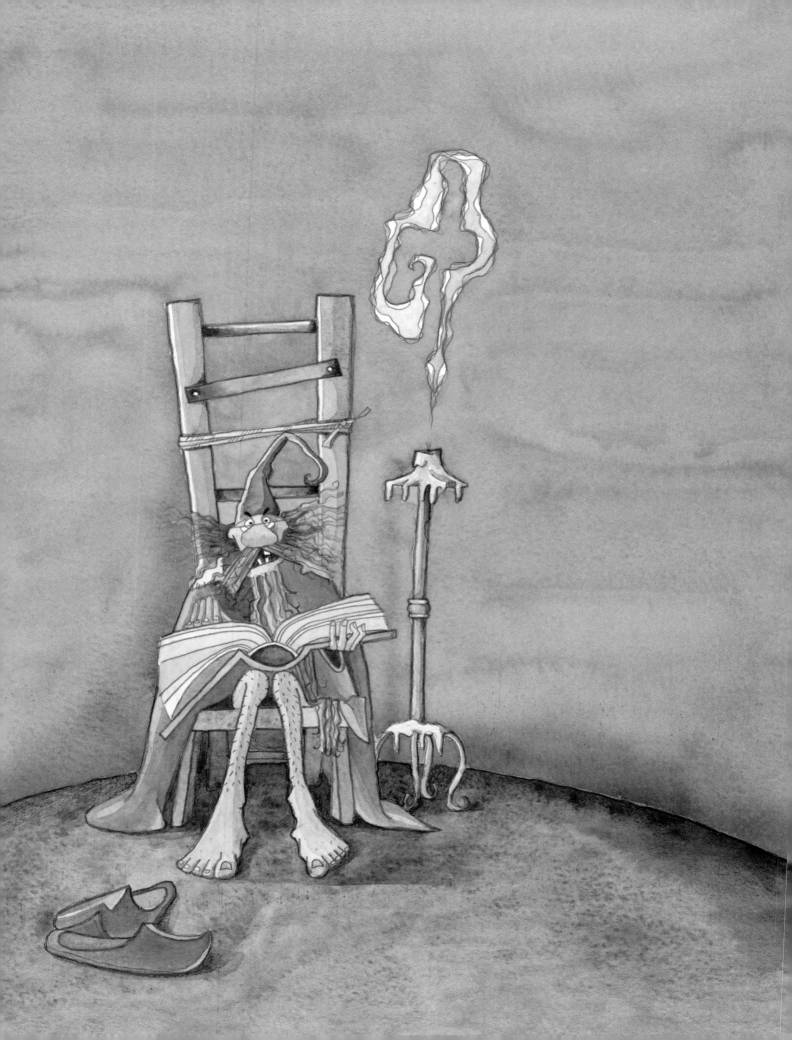

Finn shook his head.

'As the fish cooked I turned it over and burned my thumb. So I put it in my mouth – that was all!'

'You have tasted the Salmon of Wisdom!' Finegas told him. 'We may as well share it between us, for you have made the old prophecy come true – that he who first tastes the Salmon of Wisdom possesses all the knowledge his mind can hold. I can teach you nothing, for you know more than I do. And now you will leave me.'

But before Finn went he finished the chair and carved every bit of it, so that when Finegas sat there and dozed, wonderful dreams came to him and he was happy.

'Lucky I was to have known Finn in his youth,' said the poet. 'But luckier still if he could have stayed with me!'

Finn and the Goblin

Before going to study poetry and wisdom with Finegas, Finn had left his weapons with Bobdall and Luacha. He went back to collect them and to see if his old friends were happy. He knew before he came near their home that they had used the jewels he had given them wisely and generously. There were dwellings in every clearing. He found a ford at the stream. The woodcutter's axe and the hammer at the forge sent their music through the forest.

Luacha saw him coming and caught her breath.

'You have gained great knowledge,' she said. 'I did not understand how learned that old poet must be.'

'He caught the Salmon of Wisdom and I ate it,' he told her.

'You were always the one for fish!' chuckled Bobdall.

Finn smiled. They seemed younger than he remembered. He felt older and thought kindly of them, as if they were children.

'Where are you going?' asked Luacha, for she knew he could not stay with them.

'He is going where he will become Chief of the Fianna!' declared Bobdall.

Finn set off for Tara.

He arrived there during the Great Assembly, when neither fighting nor quarrelling was allowed, and sat behind the Fianna. Soon he was asked his name.

'I am Finn, son of Cool, and I have come to serve the King as my father did.'

The King was pleased with this tall, serious young man and welcomed him. So did the Fianna. But he was the youngest there and they could not know he was determined to become their Chief.

That summer, a goblin came during the night and blew fire against the palace. There were guards along the walls, but the demon brought his harp with him and played so sweetly, the men stood still while fire streamed over their heads. In the morning as they stirred and looked around they saw blackened ruins.

The palace and walls were rebuilt and the King promised wealth and land

to anyone who could overcome the goblin. Even Goll of Clan Morna and Chief of the Fianna could not resist that music. But Finn knew he must try.

He went to the King. 'If I slay the Fire Demon, shall I have my father's place as head of the Fianna?' he asked.

'If you succeed, no man would dare refuse you!' answered the King.

When the warriors heard this, one of them who had been with Finn's father, Cool, brought him a magic spear of bronze and Arabian gold. He gave this to Finn, telling him that when he heard the first notes of the goblin's harp, he must lay the naked blade against his forehead.

'Then you may resist the Demon,' he said.

Finn demanded that he should be the only one to guard Tara that night and the King agreed. As darkness came, he stood on the ramparts, watching. Out of a mist which spread over the plain he saw a small, dark form arise and come towards him.

A single lovely note came from the Magic Harp and Finn felt his spirit flying from his body. He longed to follow it so that he might come nearer to that wonderful music. His head drooped and rested against the cool blade of the spear. Slowly his spirit returned. The music swelled about him but, before one flame could be flung at Tara, he leaped from the wall.

The goblin fled through the mist, with Finn

after him. The King, warriors, and all the people of the court crowded the ramparts. They saw a dark shadow, outlined with fire, speed over the plain, Finn racing after it. Both passed out of sight.

The goblin had almost reached the fairy rath of Slieve Fuad when Finn caught up with him, killed him with the Magic Spear and, cutting off his head, carried it in triumph back to Tara.

Chief of the Fianna

King Cormac kept his promise and proclaimed Finn Chief of the Fianna. Goll was the first to swear obedience to him and all the others followed. So Finn won his father's place and all through his life the Fianna upheld the honour of Ireland.

Some of the maxims Finn taught are written in the old books:

> *In the house be quiet; be surly in the narrow pass.*
>
> *Do not beat your hound unless he is at fault.*
>
> *Do not meddle with a buffoon, for he is but a fool.*
>
> *Be gentle to women, to children and to poets, and never be violent to the common people.*
>
> *Do not swagger, or boast, or take part in a brawl.*
>
> *As long as you live, do not forsake your chief for gold or any reward in the world.*
>
> *Never abandon one you are pledged to protect.*

A chief should not abuse his people.

Do not bear tales, or tell falsehoods.

Never stir up strife.

Do not frequent the drinking house or find fault with the old.

Give food freely.

Hold fast to your arms.

Finn was the greatest captain the Fianna ever had. He gave away his gold and everything he possessed to those who needed it and he was more ready to protect the weak than to fight for glory. He ruled his warriors wisely and never bore a grudge.

Conan, son of Lia, who had been killed by Finn, had never forgiven his father's death. When Finn became Chief, Conan abandoned the Fianna and for seven years was an outlaw, raiding cattle, setting fire to houses, killing men and hounds.

The Fianna traced him to Carn Lewy in Munster. But they could not find his hiding place. Finn sat resting, when Conan came up on him from behind and flung his long sinewy arms about him. Finn guessed who was holding him and did not move.

'What do you want, now that you can no longer escape?' he asked. 'In spite of my enmity with your father, I have no wish to kill you.'

'Since it is the only thing left for me to do, let me take service with you,' replied Conan.

Finn laughed.

'Come back to the Fianna, Conan, and if you will keep faith so will I!'

And Conan served him faithfully for thirty years, to the end of his life.

There was another Conan – Conan Mac Morna, nicknamed the Bald – who had a bitter, mocking tongue. He was a big fat man with a bald head, and as greedy and grudging as Finn was generous. Everyone knew that underneath his tunic, his skin was covered with thick, black wool. But not everyone knew the way it had happened to him.

One day, when some of the Fianna were out hunting, they came to a part of the forest where they had never been before. A broad, white road led to an open glade and there before them they saw a grand mansion with glistening walls and a high, green roof. Wondering who could live there, they raised a shout, asking if they might enter. Not a sound answered them, but their own voices echoing among the trees. The door stood open, so they went in slowly and treading softly. The place was empty but, in the centre of the hall, the table was laid for a feast, with

boiled and roast meat hot and steaming. A silver cup of red wine stood by each plate. They sat down and ate and drank, for they were all hungry.

One of the Fianna, looking up from his plate, saw the wall in front of him, which had been hung with silk-embroidered curtains, change to rough, bare tree trunks. Startled, he looked up and discovered the ceiling growing lower and lower, while the walls were closing in on them.

With a cry of warning he sprang to his feet, spilling the wine in his cup and sending his seat crashing to the floor.

'We're enchanted!' he said and his voice shook with fear. He rushed to the door, the other warriors crowding after him.

Only Conan the Bald still sat at the table. He was as afraid as the others, but he had never enjoyed such venison or such sparkling wine and he determined not to move until he had finished every bit on his plate.

But when he saw the last few men squeeze through the narrowing door-way, he tried to stand up and follow. To his horror, he discovered he was stuck fast in his chair.

'I can't get up!' he shouted. 'Don't leave me, comrades! Help me out!'

Two looked back, saw his trouble and rushed to him, seized his arms, tugged and tugged until they had him out of the chair. But his clothes, and his skin with them, were left sticking to the wood.

All they could do was to wrap him in a fresh sheepskin, which a shepherd on the hill outside gave them. This grew onto his flesh so that he was always clothed in wool.

Keelta, another of Finn's companions, lived on when the rest of the Fianna were dead. He became so old that he met St Patrick and told the saint stories of the ancient times. After he became a Christian and was baptised, he would sit talking to St Patrick while a scribe wrote down every word he said.

'They were pagans!' declared the scribe bitterly.

'They were men we can learn from. Tell me more about the Fianna,' said Patrick.

'They weren't just fighters,' explained Keelta. 'Nowadays they'd call them learned scholars. A man couldn't join the Fianna until he knew the Twelve Books of Poetry. He must be able to make good verses and recite the deeds and stories of his race before the bards and poets.

'If they said he'd done well, then he'd be put into a hole up to his middle. Armed with only shield and hazel wand, he'd have to defend himself against nine warriors with spears. If one of them scratched him, he could not join the Fianna.

'For the next test, his hair was twisted into small plaits and he was chased through the forest. If he was caught, if one plait came untwisted, if as he ran a dry twig cracked under his foot, he could not join the Fianna.

'When all these tests were passed, he would be expected to leap over a pole held as high as his head, to run at full speed under a rod at the level of his knee and draw out a thorn from his foot while running. Then he could join the Fianna!'

The Chase on Slieve Gallion

Finn had two hounds, Bran and Skolawn. They were more than dogs to him: they were friends and companions. They weren't ordinary hounds and their eyes were not the eyes of dogs but of human beings. Tyren, Finn's aunt, had been changed by a spell into a hound, and Bran and Skolawn were her children.

Finn was hunting with them by the Hill of Allen when they started a fawn and followed it to the top of Slieve Gallion, where the fawn disappeared beyond a silver birch. There Finn came upon a woman wrapped in a long silk cloak with gleaming jewels in her hair and around her neck. She sat by a lake, tears streaming down her cheeks. Finn asked her why she wept.

'My ring has dropped in the lake, my lovely ring!' she answered. 'And I put a **geis** upon you to dive into the lake and find it for me.'

Finn obeyed. But he had to dive many times before he found the ring. As he pulled himself to the bank and handed it to the woman, without a word of thanks, she plunged into the water.

Finn tried to spring after her, but he was so weak he stumbled and fell. He lay there, unable to rise, changed into a feeble old man with long, white hair.

Even his own hounds did not know him, but ran round and round trying to track their lost master and whining unhappily.

When Finn did not return, some of the Fianna went in search of him. They traced his footsteps and the light prints of the hounds up to the lake where Bran and Skolawn ran to them frantically.

Keelta asked the old man who was lying there had the great Finn passed that way. The trembling creature answered so faintly that Keelta had to bend close.

'I am Finn!' he heard.

Keelta started. But here Finn had come and here he had disappeared. So he listened patiently.

Finn told what had happened and the Fianna guessed the cause of his misfortune. The fawn must have come from the Fairy Mound of Slieve Gallion.

They carried Finn to his home. Others, led by Keelta, began to dig a tunnel into the mound. Day and night they toiled until they reached an underground cavern.

A tall girl stood there holding a golden goblet of wine, which she handed to Keelta without saying one word. Keelta hurried back and gave it to Finn. They watched anxiously while he drank. With each sip his cheeks filled out and were stained with colour, his eyes grew bright and his limbs straightened; his clenched fists were as strong as ever.

Only his hair remained white. He could have changed it with another goblet of wine from the Fairy Mound and Keelta was eager to return for it. But Finn would not allow this and his hair remained white for the rest of his life.

The Hard Gilly

The Fianna had been hunting over the hills of Desmond (Munster) and Finn stood listening to the horns and cries of the hounds when he saw a tall, ugly man dragging by the halter a mare as ugly and ungainly as himself. The man's shield was battered and dingy, his sword rusty, his tunic dirty and tattered.

'Who are you?' demanded Finn. 'Where do you come from and what do you want?'

'I am Dacar, the Hard Gilly,' replied the man. 'I come from over the sea and I want to serve under you, Finn Mac Cool. But listen to my warning – I am the hardest servant a master ever had and I eat as much as one hundred ordinary men.'

'We can but try,' said Finn, laughing. 'How will you serve me?'

'Who is paid the best among the Fianna, a horseman or a footman?' asked the Hard Gilly.

'A horseman,' Finn told him. 'He has twice as much pay as a footman.'

'Then I'll be a horseman in your service, Finn Mac Cool!' declared the man.

He pulled away the halter and his mare rushed among the horses, biting and kicking until the whole troop were fighting and screaming like mad creatures.

'Take away your mare!' cried Conan Mac Morna. 'Finn has made many bad bargains, but this is the worst.'

'I'm no horse boy!' said the Hard Gilly proudly. 'I will not bring out the mare!'

Fearing that all the horses would be injured, Conan flung a halter over the mare's head and leaped on her back. At once she stood still, her head drooping, looking more wretched than ever.

She was so long that, for a joke, thirteen of the Fianna scrambled up behind Conan and still there wasn't a move from the mare.

'I'll not stay to be mocked!' cried the Hard Gilly indignantly. 'I'll leave your service before I enter it Finn Mac Cool!' and he stumbled away, looking so disreputable, Finn was thankful to see him going.

Suddenly the Gilly began to run. He did not seem to move quickly, yet he covered the ground like a swift horse. The mare, with Conan and his thirteen companions clinging to one another, raced after her master, who kept on until he came to the Kerry shore. There he leaped into the sea, the mare and her riders following.

Finn and the rest of the Fianna arrived in time to see them disappear. Liagan, the swiftest runner of them all shot ahead and seized hold of the mare's tail as she went under.

'What shall we do now?' asked the Fianna crowding round Finn.

'We must rescue them!' decided Finn. 'And, as I'd sooner be on the sea than under it, we'll furnish a boat and start as soon as we can.'

When the boat was ready, Finn and several of the Fianna went on

board and hoisted the sail. In a few days wind and tides brought them to a mountainous island. Towering cliffs rose sheer from the shore and they could discover no way of landing. But Dermot O'Dyna determined to climb up and discover what lay beyond the cliffs.

Slowly he pulled himself up the bare rock, not daring to look down. He could find no way of bringing the others after him, so he turned inland through a tangled wood. He crossed a stream and came to a well, shadowed by a great tree from which hung a beautiful drinking horn. Dermot took down the horn, for he was hot and thirsty. As he dipped it in the well, the water surged and rose in a column which threatened to fall on him.

He drank three times and, as he put back the horn, an angry man came striding through the wood, shouting insults and boasting that while he was Champion of the Well, no stranger should drink from it.

'You're a strange warrior to deny a wanderer a drink of water!' retorted Dermot contemptuously.

The champion leaped on him and they fought for hours. Dermot was forcing the other back when he twisted away and jumped into the well.

Dermot made a fire, ate some food he had brought with him and lay down to sleep. In the morning he found the champion standing guard over the well and once more they fought. As darkness came the champion leaped into the well and left Dermot alone in the night.

The third day it happened as on the first two days. But, as the champion was about to leap into the well, Dermot flung his arms about him and they went in together.

The young man fell into a deep sleep and when he awoke, he was lying on a grassy bank. A tall, armed man was standing over him. With a friendly smile he helped Dermot to his feet and told him he was in the country of the King of Sorca. They went to a castle where Dermot found his friends who had been carried off on the Hard Gilly's mare.

They could not explain why they were there. They were feasted and entertained, but when they asked why they had been so tricked, the men of the Fianna could get no answer.

While Dermot was climbing the cliff, Finn sailed the boat farther along the coast and found a cove where they landed easily. They went along the cliffs and followed Dermot's tracks as far as the well. From there they wandered through a forest and came to a huge cavern, opening on the hillside above the castle, where Dermot and the lost men of the Fianna were being held.

Finn led the way down the hill. But the gates of the castle were opened and the King of Sorca stood there to welcome them. Before they would enter, Finn demanded an explanation and the Fianna stood around listening.

'The Champion of the Well is my enemy,' said the King. 'He is always making war upon my people and attacking this castle. He grows stronger every day. So I determined to bring the Fianna of Erin here to help me. I am the Hard Gilly and it's true I brought you and your men here by a trick. But I could think of no other way. Say, Finn Mac Cool, will you fight with the people of Sorca?'

'I have never yet refused a request!' declared Finn. 'Nor will I now, though you gave my men a hard ride, Gilly Dacar!'

In the land of Sorca, they had never seen such fighters. The Fianna drove their foe before them and the battle was ended before even Conan the Bald was weary. Peace was made between the King of Sorca and the Champion of the Well.

'What reward can I give you for saving my kingdom?' asked the King.

'It should be a good reward,' muttered Conan greedily. 'We fought well and there are many of us to share it.'

'The wage I paid you when you were a Gilly in my service, and that is nothing,' Finn told the King. 'And now we must return to Erin.'

'Look at your men, Finn Mac Cool!' said the King of Sorca.

Finn turned and saw his men, but they and he were standing not with the King of Sorca, but on the sandy shore where the Hard Gilly and his mare, with the fifteen Fianna clinging to her, had plunged beneath the waves.

The Kingdom of the Dwarfs

A Strange Story

There was always feasting in Faylinn. Iubdan, who was king there in the time of Conor Mac Nessa, loved music and singing. So he celebrated victories and birthdays as well as the usual festivals. He welcomed strangers and, if but one arrived, he would order a banquet.

The people of Faylinn were very, very small, but proud and sure of their fame, though, at that time, no one in Ireland had heard of them. And Iubdan was the proudest of them all!

It was the harvest season and Iubdan sat at the top table, watching the serving girls pass along the benches with brimming jugs as tall as themselves to fill the drinking horns, while men carried dishes of steaming food.

Iubdan was happy. The storehouses were full and the honey drink was the strongest and sweetest he had tasted for years. He raised his speckled horn bound with gold and engraved with leaping salmon.

'Did you ever hear tell of a better king than meself?' he shouted.

'We never did!' roared the feasters, for Iubdan was a kind, generous ruler and if he were given to boasting – who minded that?

Iubdan's horn was filled again and a shower of golden drops sparkled on the polished board as he drank the health of Glower, the strongest man in Faylinn, who sat just below the royal table.

'Did you ever hear tell of a strong man that is the equal of the strong man of Faylinn?' demanded Iubdan.

'We did not!' they cried.

Glower was so good-natured not one of them feared him, though he could hew down a thistle with one stroke of his axe and had been known to wrestle with twelve men, one after the other, laying each man flat on his back.

'By our word, we have never heard of a better man!' they shouted, and all the men

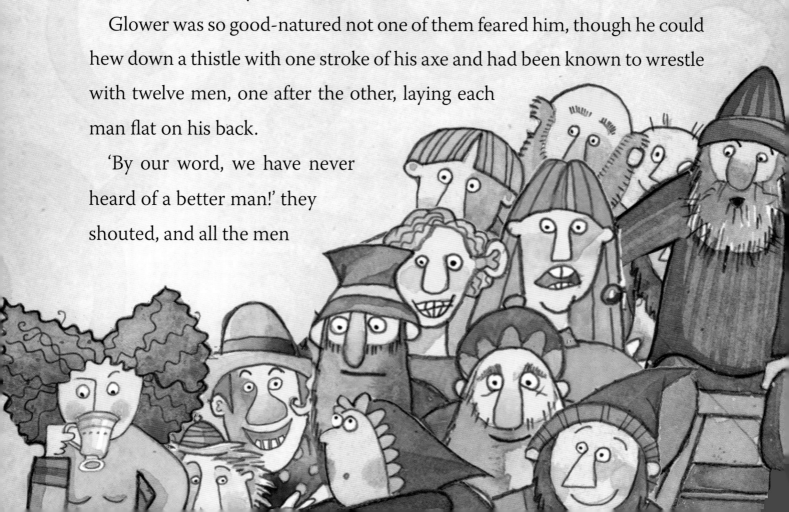

and women sitting in the banqueting hall raised their horns to Glower.

'Were there ever horses or fighting men swifter and braver than ours?' went on King Iubdan.

'Indeed no,' agreed the feasters, not so loudly this time, for the wine of Faylinn was strong and comforting.

Iubdan continued his bragging speech.

'It would be a hard task to take captives or hostages from this land, so brave, so fierce, so numerous are the haughty fighters of our race. They are the men who become kings in other lands!'

A burst of laughter answered the little King. He was so startled he almost dropped the speckled horn and some of the drink spattered the Queen's crimson robe.

He stared about him. Opposite Glower, who was asleep, his head on the table, sat Eisirt, Chief Poet of the Court, and it was he who laughed.

'Why are you laughing?' demanded Iubdan.

Eisirt put his hands on the table and stood up so that everyone could see him.

'I have heard of a land where the people are so big and brave that one man could take hostages and captives from four of our battalions.'

Iubdan drained his horn and handed it to a serving man.

'Seize him!' he ordered the guards, pointing to Eisirt. 'Put chains on him and carry him to the deepest dungeon!'

As Eisirt was being marched away, Bebo, the Queen, who had fallen asleep, rubbed her eyes.

'What are they doing with the Poet?' she asked. 'And who spilled drink over my best robe?'

'He mocked and insulted me!' growled the King. 'How could I help spilling a drop of honey wine?'

Bebo shook her head.

'That's very strange. Eisirt is always polite to me. What did he say?'

Iubdan told her. She listened in amazement.

'You put a Poet in prison – the Chief Poet!' she exclaimed. 'That is not wise. And for such a wonderful story! Bring him back. I want to hear more.'

Iubdan was ashamed of his bad temper. He gave the order and back came Eisirt.

He was cross, for his feelings had been hurt. Bebo poured him two horns of wine before he would tell them any more. By this time, the strong man and all the other sleepers were roused, and they listened with startled eyes to the wonders Eisirt told them.

'The lad I had it from – a seafaring chap with a deal of experience and hardship behind him – said the men in this far country are as tall as our tallest trees!' declared the Poet. 'Their horses are monsters and the palaces of their chiefs are vast hollow mountains. In that land the bees are bigger than eagles and the grass is as high as this table!'

He thumped the polished wood with his tiny clenched fist.

'What is the name of this country?' asked Bebo curiously and, forgetting her manners, she put her elbows on the table.

'They call it Ireland, ma'am!' replied Eisirt with a bow, for he nearly always remembered his manners.

'How far away is it?'

'In a straight line it would take at least fourteen days to ride there and back, your Majesty.'

Iubdan had listened in silence. Now he decided it was time to let them know he was King.

'I'll give you twice that time to go there and bring back proofs of this story of a giant race,' he announced. 'Isn't it queer I never heard tell of this marvellous country? And, mind now, if you've made it all up, never return to Faylinn!'

'Oh, Iubdan! How cruel!' cried Bebo.

But Eisirt looked boldly at the King.

'I will go, Iubdan, and I will return!'

The whole court, and most of the people who had heard of the argument and had nothing to do, gathered to see Eisirt start upon his desperate adventure. Ban, his pure white horse was waiting, its coat glossy with brushing. Its long mane and tail were braided for the journey. The bridle was hung with silver bells and the saddle of yellow leather gleamed in the sunlight. Eisirt looked grand indeed in his gold embroidered tunic, his scarlet cloak and his white shoes sewn with pearls.

'Take care of yourself!' called Queen Bebo.

'Remember me orders!' said Iubdan. 'No proof, no return!'

'I'll return!' answered Eisirt, without a glance backward.

A Terrible Journey

He shook the reins and, as the silver bells tinkled, light as a butterfly, the fairy steed pranced down the path to the palace gates. The crowds inside and out cheered, the Queen waved her blue silk handkerchief, but Iubdan stood still and silent.

'It's going to be mighty dull,' he thought, 'without that boyo's songs and stories.'

'I'll be after him!' cried Glower, the strong man, running towards the open gates.

'Come back!' shouted the King.

Glower returned slowly, frowning and indignant.

''Tis a disgrace to let our Poet go alone among giants!' he muttered. 'He needs a comrade. I should be with him. Once he praised my strength in a song.'

'Isn't it bad enough to see the last of our best poet without losing me strong man too?' asked Iubdan laughing.

Eisirt, the Poet, heard the cheers until he came to the cliff which guarded the shores of Faylinn. Before him lay the sea. The wind was fresh and damp with spray. Eisirt trembled as he watched the white-tipped crests of the waves surging as far as he could see.

'Wouldn't you think an odd dozen or so would have come with me this far,' he grumbled. 'Not one of them would take the trouble. Not even Glower. I thought better of him. And I hate all that water. There's too much of it!'

His horse, weary of standing still, stamped, tossed its head and whinnied.

Eisirt smiled.

'Now, my noble horse,' he said, 'show what a Poet's steed can do. If only you had wings I wouldn't be trembling the way I am.'

Once more he shook the reins and, at the silver tinkle, the tiny horse leaped out upon the air, spread its legs and neighed fearlessly.

Each time a tossing wave touched its hoofs Eisirt shuddered, but Ban bounded along as though it galloped across a meadow.

The Poet dared not look down. He was stiff and hungry. He began to yawn and his eyes were half closed.

'I mustn't fall asleep,' he told himself. 'I can't swim and if I fall into the sea I'll be drowned. Why did I set out on this foolish journey? Who cares if there are giants in the world?'

A great wave swelled beneath them. The little horse leaped higher than ever and this time came down upon firm, yellow sand.

Eisirt was so delighted they had crossed the sea he opened his mouth to sing. But a thick, white mist came rolling up, hiding sea and land and setting him coughing. With his hand on the horse's mane, he groped his way up to the rocks and, where two leaned against each other, he spread the saddle-cloth upon a heap of dry seaweed, propped the saddle against the rock for a pillow, stretched himself out, with his cloak tucked over his knees, and opened the saddle bags.

Queen Bebo had packed them herself, so there was plenty. Eisirt opened a bottle of honey wine and drank half without taking his mouth away. He poured the rest down the tired horse's throat. Next he drew out a meat pasty, with onions and herbs in it and jelly so thick and tasty Eisirt was vexed he couldn't see it properly.

Then the two of them slept, Ban lying before the opening to protect his master in that strange land.

Once Eisirt woke and saw the moonlight streaming through the mist. He longed to make a poem about it, but fell asleep again before he could think of the correct rhymes.

In the morning a wind was tearing at the mist. The sun was so pale it looked like another moon. All day they rode where monstrous animals with grinning teeth and curved horns dashed across a vast plain. Enormous trees blocked the way, rocks towered above them, threatening to fall. But as Eisirt rode up to them, they dissolved into wavering clouds. The Poet, knowing they had come to the Land of Mist, kept straight on until his feet were stiff in the stirrups, his hands cold and tired with clutching the reins. The following day they came out of the mist and raced over a wild bog. As the sun rose and their shadows kept company with them, Eisirt felt less lonely. Still he dared not sing.

He forgot how many days and nights he had journeyed from Faylinn. When he slept, he dreamed of happy feasts and woke to find a bitter wind tossing the soft white tips of the bog cotton.

'I'd almost be glad to meet a giant,' he muttered as they crouched under a clump of heather. 'I never could stand lonesomeness!'

The wind died. The sun turned the pools to gold and the heather had so many shades of purple, Eisirt shared the last of the honey drink and a plum cake.

'A feast's a feast,' he said to the little horse. 'If there's not a crumb left, it means we'll find food somewhere. Only let's get through this wonderful forest.'

For the bushes seemed like great trees to him.

When the real trees rose upon the horizon, Eisirt watched for them to fade as the trees of mist had faded. But the nearer he came to them, the taller and stronger they appeared and he closed his eyes hoping they would disappear.

But when he looked again they were still there.

Brave Ban no longer galloped. His head drooped, his mane and tail trailed in the dust of the path they followed.

Eisirt too was weary. He longed for home.

'I always did like a story of wanderings and strange happenings,' he said. 'But I never wanted to go straying through the world. And me and me poor little horse have to go through this because Iubdan couldn't keep from boasting. Does no one live in this desolate country?'

How long had he been riding – years, weeks, or only days? Suddenly he heard the music of a horn!

Three times it called and Eisirt, wondering what he would discover, urged Ban towards the sound.

Along the stony track the little horse trotted eagerly. At last lights and the glow of fires shone above them in the darkening air.

On a patch of young grass in the shelter of a high bank the horse stopped. Eisirt slipped to the ground.

'Mebbe ye're right,' he whispered. 'I'm not equal to facing what's before me till I've had a rest. Ah, if only I'd a bite and sup.'

Shouts of men and the lowing of cattle were all about them. A low-growing elder tree concealed the travellers and the poet was thankful, for the men who passed and the animals they herded were indeed giants. For all his courage, he was afraid.

Now he heard the clanging of heavy gates and they were once more alone.

A woman, overburdened, had dropped a creel of dried grass and forgotten it. Here was shelter against wind and cold. Searching in the saddlebags, Eisirt found some hard crusts he had left and one of the bottles still held a few mouthfuls of wine. Curling up snugly he slept until the rising sun wakened him with its warmth.

He lay listening to Ban crunching grass, a stalk at a time, and half-welcomed, half-dreaded the coming day.

Ban, hearing his master moving, came nearer and blowing cheerfully, bent down to rub Eisirt's head with his soft nose.

Eisirt sat up.

'This is the most important day in our lives,' he declared. 'If we fail to enter and make friends, we will be wanderers always. If we succeed we will be famous and our deeds will be written in golden ink in the Annals of Faylinn!'

Ban whinnied and tossed his head.

'What do you hear?' asked the poet. 'There are great birds in the trees. Is it the opening of doors and the rattling of pots? My word, but I'm famished!'

He sprang to his feet, looked up and saw at the top of the earthen bank a stone wall pierced by a great wooden gate.

He combed his hair, smoothed his clothes, groomed Ban with a handful of dried grass, mounted and drew out his Poet's wand.

A path beaten flat by feet and hoofs led steeply to the gate.

'We must have the gates opened for us!' declared Eisirt. 'If those giants and their animals come swarming out before they know we are here we shall be destroyed.'

When they reached the gate, without dismounting, he beat on it with his wand.

A sleepy guard took down the bar and, holding his spear in readiness, opened the gate a crack and peeped out.

Inside the Fort of the Giants

At first the guard could see nothing, but the dew rising in fine mist from the grass at the foot of the bank and a lark singing as it began to spiral, up, up, up!

Then he heard a voice crying out: 'Tell your master, the Chief Poet of Faylinn seeks audience.'

The guard looked about him and shook his head in bewilderment. A blow on his ankle made him look down. He saw Eisirt and dropped his spear.

'Don't be afraid,' the Poet told him. 'Go immediately to your master and I'll do you no harm.'

The guard closed the gate and, wrinkling his nose in wonder, hurried towards the King's chamber.

Fergus Mac Leda, King of Emania in Ulster, had passed a troubled night and was standing in the doorway of the banqueting hall thinking over his dreams, when the guard came running.

'Listen, Chief!' he said. 'There's a wee man at the gate asking for you. He's the height of the world for grandeur and he's no taller than your knee.'

'Bring him to me!' ordered Fergus and entering the hall, he strode to his seat at the high table.

The nobles, some yawning, came hurrying in. The Queen, with her women, was not long after. So that when the guard returned, carrying Eisirt upon his open hand and the little horse under his arm, the morning feast had begun.

Fergus, lifting his drinking cup, put it down untasted when he saw the tiny Poet, dressed in magnificent clothes, gazing at him without the least sign of fear.

'By my sword!' cried the King. 'You are welcome to our Court! Eda! I thought you a dwarf. Stop eating and salute your rival.'

Eda was the smallest man seen before in Emania. But he was a giant to the stranger from Faylinn.

'I am not only a dwarf,' he said proudly. 'I am a bard!'

'I am a Poet!' retorted Eisirt. 'I make my own verses. You but sing those of other men.'

'You are a stranger,' said Eda with a low bow. 'And at the Court of Fergus poets are as welcome as bards or warriors, and sometimes I make my own verses.'

'Well said!' cried the King. 'You are indeed welcome, noble Poet. Eat and drink and, when you are rested, tell us your name and country.'

Eisirt was thankful to sit beside Eda, drink from a toy cup, eat thick porridge, scraps of roast meat and crushed hazelnut cake.

Eda smiled at the strange Poet and kept his cup and plate filled.

'I never thought to meet a man smaller than myself,' he said. 'And that man a maker of poems.'

'Will Ban, my horse, be safe?' asked Eisirt. 'He's the only friend I have in these parts.'

'You have me for friend and comrade!' declared Eda. 'But I'll see your horse is well cared for.'

He was back before Eisirt had finished eating.

'That's a grand steed!' he said. 'He's in the Grianan and the Queen's youngest daughter is combing his mane with her silver comb.'

Eisirt pushed away his platter and cup.

'I'm ready now, and willing,' he told them, 'for you all to hear my story.'

The Chief Poet of Faylinn sat on a cushion at King Fergus' elbow, the nobles crowding round and as many serving men and women and warriors as could squeeze into the hall.

There wasn't a sound from them as Eisirt told of Iubdan's boasting, of his own knowledge that a race of giants lived in Ireland and of the task laid upon him to bring back proof.

'What proof is possible, unfortunate Poet?' asked the Queen kindly.

Eisirt shook his head. He didn't know.

'I'll be the proof!' declared Eda. 'I'll go with my new friend and convince his King. We bards and poets must stand by one another.'

Then Eisirt recited his best poems and made one in praise of the hospitable and courteous giants of Emania.

Fergus and the Queen had never had a visitor they liked better. But Eisirt was homesick and was under bond to return quickly to Faylinn. The King gave him a bag of gold. The Queen presented him with a gold chain set with purple stones and mussel pearls. Eisirt shared the gold among the servants. The chain he clasped round his waist for it was too big and heavy to wear round his neck. So he and Eda set off for Faylinn.

Eisirt rode and the dwarf ran beside him. They went a far shorter way than the Poet had taken, and the land he had thought so deserted seemed filled with forts and settlements, where both were welcomed and entertained. When they reached the shore a boat was ready for them. Without sail or oar it skimmed over the water so swiftly that Eisirt was amazed when the cliffs towered above them and he knew they had reached his own country.

They climbed to the top and Eda carried Eisirt the last half.

'Welcome to Faylinn!' cried the Poet.

Proof

Eisirt sat proudly on his horse, with Eda marching beside him. The dwarf stared curiously at the tiny people ploughing fields no bigger than a banquet table and at the gaily coloured houses scattered like forgotten toys.

'Hark at the shouting!' cried Eisirt. 'The whole countryside will greet you. Only why are they running away? That's very strange!'

Eda laughed.

'They're terrified, the poor wee things. But what's that they're calling me? A Fomorian giant! Fomorian indeed! And me a good Ulsterman!'

His face was red. He was angry now.

'Don't be vexed,' pleaded Eisirt. 'They're poor simple people who aren't travelled like us. They've never been away from Faylinn. They know nothing of foreign parts. When they get used to you, they'll be crowding round, cheering. And look! Yonder come the King and Queen! They've never before been this far to welcome a stranger!'

The royal horses were so frightened they reared and neighed. Like the people, they thought Eda a giant. But Iubdan was the bravest man in the country, except Eisirt, and Bebo, the Queen, wouldn't let anyone know she was shaking with terror.

'Welcome, giant from Emania!' said Iubdan, managing to speak in a friendly voice. 'If there are more of you in that place, you must be a great people.'

'I am a dwarf in Ulster!' declared Eda. 'Our warriors are all over six feet high and a child of seven or eight would be my size.'

'You'd be welcome whatever your size,' said Iubdan. 'Especially as you bring back our Poet.'

'Very welcome,' added Bebo. But she spoke in a trembling voice.

'We'll have a feast!' decided Iubdan, and at once he was happy.

He ordered twice as much honey wine, roast meat, apples and cakes as for an ordinary feast.

'We may be small,' he told Eisirt, 'but I'll show this Fomorian giant we're as generous as the best in Emania.'

'He's not a giant!' protested Eisirt. 'And he isn't a Fomorian.'

But he was delighted to be once more feasting in Faylinn.

It was the grandest feast ever known in Faylinn. Just when everyone was feeling friendly and Eda was telling the King he didn't want to go back to Emania for a long time, Eisirt stood up.

They knew he was not giving a toast for his horn lay empty on the table before him. He folded his arms and looked straight at Iubdan.

'When I told you of the Land of Giants, where men are taller than trees, bees are like eagles, palaces mountains, you would not believe me. You demanded proof. I journeyed to Ulster in Ireland and this noble Eda came back with me to prove I had told the truth.'

'And he's very welcome!' declared Iubdan, raising his horn to Eda and draining it to the last drop.

Eisirt frowned. He did not like being interrupted, even by the King.

'In his own country,' he went on, 'Eda is a dwarf. Now I put you under geis, King Iubdan, to go to Emania, as I have done, enter the Fort of King Fergus and taste his porridge.'

Iubdan was dismayed. The geis was the bond of chivalry which no chieftain of Faylinn or of Ireland could refuse without being shamed.

He wished he had believed Eisirt from the beginning. He wished he had not put the Poet in prison or dreamed of forcing him to go to Ulster. He wished he had never heard of the Land of Giants!

But he had to go or be disgraced forever.

'You've brought this on yourself!' Queen Bebo told him. 'You'd no right to treat Eisirt the way you did. But no one can make you hear reason. Now you'll have to go among strangers and giants at that. But I'll go with you.'

'You'll like Emania,' Eda the dwarf told her.

How Iubdan kept the Geis

Iubdan had a magic steed which could travel over sea as easily as over land. It was the biggest in all Faylinn and carried the King and Queen comfortably. They would have liked Eda to go with them, but Iubdan was ashamed to ask him. Bebo had invited the dwarf to stay in Faylinn as long as he wished, so she couldn't say a word. Off they went and at long last they reached the Fort of Fergus.

Their journey had been much easier than Eisirt's, for they had his experience and Eda's advice to help them. But they were every bit as frightened when they arrived as night came and the gates were being closed. In the scurry and confusion of the crowd who feared they would be shut out, the little people and their horse entered without being seen.

They hid behind the royal stable until the torches were dimmed in the great hall. Then in they crept, the horse with them, for Iubdan wouldn't be parted from it for a moment in this huge, strange place.

The fire was still glowing. Great logs, half-burned, threw a red light across the floor, but the upper part of the hall was in darkness.

'Everything is so big,' whispered Bebo. 'I wish we were back in Faylinn.'

'One taste of the porridge and we'll be away before daybreak,' Iubdan whispered back.

Bebo thought of the monstrous gates.

'When will they be opened?' she wondered.

Cauldrons as big as Faylinn rooms were drawn back from the hearth and Iubdan tapped each one with his sword.

'They're all empty,' he grumbled.

But the last gave out a dull, heavy sound.

'There's something in this,' said Iubdan.

'It's the porridge pot sure enough!' declared Bebo. 'There's lumps of it on the outside. Thick, nasty stuff. The scullions must be very dirty and lazy. If I were Queen here – !'

'Hush!' said Iubdan. 'Help me up!'

They led the horse close to the pot, and with Bebo's help, Iubdan scrambled to its back. By standing on tip-toe, he managed to reach the rim and pulled himself up.

'Hand me the spoon!' he said.

The spoon with the long handle from their own kitchen was strapped to the saddle. Bebo unfastened the buckles and held it up.

Iubdan seized it cautiously, held on to the rim of the pot with one hand and reached down for a spoonful of porridge.

Suddenly, with a shout of surprise, he toppled over and landed feet downwards in the thick, cold stuff.

Luckily he clutched the spoon. It lay on top of the porridge and kept him from sinking. But he could not get out.

Bebo climbed onto the horse's back and looked down upon Iubdan. When she saw him stuck fast with only his head showing, she screamed in terror.

'Wouldn't it be better to give me a hand and pull me out, instead of screeching and roaring!' he exclaimed. 'I'm ashamed of you. Have a little dignity, woman!'

'Dignity!' retorted Bebo. 'There's not much dignity about yourself at this moment. If you weren't so fat and heavy I might pull you out. What can I do!'

''Tis that Eisirt has us landed in this fix!' grumbled Iubdan. 'Wait till I get back to Faylinn. I'll teach him to put a **geis** on his King!'

'It's your own fault!' Bebo told him. 'You wouldn't believe Eisirt though you know it's dangerous to cross a poet. It's yourself has brought this trouble on us. Oh! Oh! Oh!'

Her cries and Iubdan's shouts roused two scullions who were sleeping nearby. They stood up blinking and yawning until they saw Bebo standing on the horse and clinging to the cauldron.

Bebo was terrified of them. They towered over her, staring in wonder, not sure if they still dreamed.

'King Iubdan has fallen into the porridge,' she told them. 'Pull him out at once!'

'Here's another of these wee people and a horse not much bigger than the Poet's,' said the tallest. 'And there's one in the pot.'

'Where do they come from?' asked the other.

'Do as I tell you!' commanded Bebo.

Her voice was quivering with fright, but she stood up straight and determined.

'A real Queen and a credit to Faylinn!' thought Iubdan.

The scullions were sleepy, but very kind. They picked Iubdan out, cleaned his clothes, gave him and Bebo sweet mead and nut cakes, shook up a cushion for them in a snug corner, and advised them to go to sleep.

'When the King wakes, we'll tell him you're here,' they promised. 'We had one of your people here before. Eisirt he was called. We were sorry to lose him and our famous dwarf went off as well.'

'I'll not sleep sound again until we're safe home in Faylinn!' declared Bebo.

But she was so tired from her adventures that she fell asleep before Iubdan. The horse lay on the floor beside them, as content as if he had never left his own stable.

⁂

In the morning Fergus was delighted to hear that two more of the little people were in the fort. He welcomed them with a feast which made the feasts of Faylinn seem poor indeed. The poets of Emania made poems about them, games were played in their honour, everyone gave them presents and they began to think how wise they were to go travelling.

One day Bebo felt tired of being among such big people. She longed for her friends, all her own size, her pet dog, and most of all she missed the children.

'They'll forget what we look like,' she told Iubdan. 'Besides I hate the way they treat us as toys. It's so undignified!'

'I'll talk to Fergus!' said the little King. 'He'll understand.'

'Stay a while,' said Fergus with a smile. 'You're nearly as good a Poet as Eisirt and I could listen to your stories forever.'

Iubdan was flattered, but each day he and Bebo became more and more homesick.

'When we don't return, Eisirt will wonder what's happened to us,' said Bebo. 'Then he'll find out and it won't be long before he sends a message.'

'What use will that be?' demanded Iubdan.

Bebo didn't know. But she trusted Eisirt and his friend, Glower.

'A Poet and a strong man,' murmured the King thoughtfully. 'If they're all we have to help us, we'll be here for the rest of our lives. Of course they have the hostage.'

'Hostage! What hostage?' asked Bebo.

'Eda!' replied Iubdan. 'Eda, the dwarf. Fergus thinks a deal of him.'

'He is no hostage, but a friend!' cried Bebo. 'And he's as helpless as we are. If you would only stop telling Fergus stories and making poems for him, he'd be more willing to let us go. But I believe in Eisirt. He'd do anything to help us. And he has secret powers.'

War by the Wee People

Bebo was right. When the King and Queen did not return to Faylinn, Eisirt, Glower and the principal people in the country decided to go in search of them. Eda, the dwarf of Emania, offered to show them the best way. He liked Faylinn. He and Eisirt were great friends and he knew Fergus was a very determined man.

'If he doesn't wish to let Bebo and Iubdan go, at his court they'll have to stay!' he warned Eisirt.

The little Poet shook his head.

'You know Fergus. But you don't yet know the might of the people of Faylinn. Even Iubdan doesn't know, for he has never been forced to call upon them. We may be small, but we have strange powers!'

Led by Eisirt, Glower and Eda, a great multitude went down to the narrow strand at the foot of the cliffs. The grand people started out on horses, the not-so-grand crowded into gaily painted carts and the poor people walked, or ran, or hung behind the carts and were there as soon as anyone.

When they reached the cliffs there was no difference between them. They all had to work pushing tree trunks, planks, boxes, anything that would float, over the edge and scramble down after them.

Then they built rafts. Eda worked harder and quicker than a dozen of the Faylinners put together. He was bigger and stronger, and he was worried.

'Fergus should be ashamed!' thought the dwarf indignantly. 'It's like tormenting a pack of innocent children. Only I'm sick and tired of being miscalled a giant when I'm only a dwarf I'd stay here, be their king and take care of them.'

There were so many rafts that the first were landing in Emania while the last was still trying to push away from Faylinn.

Iubdan was reciting a poem about trees whose wood must not be used for burning:

All trees are good for man and beast:
Some give the apples for the feast,
The juice that cheers as if 'twere wine,
The mast that comforts rooting swine,
The berries rich and flowers fair,
Or shelter from the sun's harsh glare.
So do not burn the apple tree,

The tree of drooping branches;

And do not burn the black-decked ash

The wood for warriors' lances;

Nor the noble willow tree

Priceless from root to trembling leaf,

With gold dust powdered in the spring,

Yet quivering with its secret grief;

And spare the fragile hazel bush,

Bearing its nuts that feed the wise;

But let the furze on open hearths

Gaily crackle, with golden flies

Darting aloft on scented smoke,

Passing away to the sullen night:

While stricken beech repels the cold

And floods the hall with warmth and light.

See the sad yew that proudly lifts –

when he was interrupted by a messenger laughing, but glancing in amazement over his shoulder, who came rushing to the great door.

The guards crossed their spears to keep him there, but he called to Fergus.

'There's an army of the Wee People marching over the plain!'

Fergus laughed.

'Let them come!' he said. 'I like these little people.'

'They t-threaten,' stammered the man.

'Are they armed with pins and needles?' asked Fergus.

'They are not armed,' said the messenger.

'Then why do you fear them?'

'They demand the return of Queen Bebo and King Iubdan. If you do not let them go –' He paused.

'I knew they'd stand by us!' whispered Bebo.

'Hush! Listen!' said Iubdan.

'If I do not!' exclaimed Fergus. 'What if I do not?'

'They threaten they will send a great plague upon the land of Emania!'

Fergus gripped the carved arms of his seat and, flinging back his head, laughed until he nearly choked.

'A race of midgets to threaten me!' he chuckled.

'There are great magicians among the people of Faylinn!' declared Iubdan. 'Why not let us go? We shall never forget the wonders and the kindness of your court. To keep us against our wish is to make us prisoners. We want to be your friends, not your enemies.'

But Fergus feared that if he agreed he would make himself ridiculous. He sent the messenger to order the tiny invaders away and mockingly said he would send his children to play with them.

He went to the gate and looked out.

As far as the forest, the plain was crowded with the people of Faylinn, calling on Fergus to release Bebo and Iubdan.

At nightfall when the cows were brought in, not one of them would give any milk. But when morning came the plain was deserted.

'Let us go,' pleaded Iubdan, 'or worse may happen.'

'Now that they see I will not yield to threats they have gone away,' Fergus told him.

'You haven't heard the last of the people of Faylinn!' Bebo warned the laughing King.

Seven days later when the reapers went to gather in the harvest, the ears of corn had been cut off and carried away without a sign of the robbers.

Now the people called on Fergus to save them from the wizardry of the Wee People. He laughed no longer, but he would not yield.

Then the wells were filled with rubbish, the streams blocked with stones. There was no longer laughter and feasting at the court of Fergus. Instead there was hunger and thirst.

Again the Wee People appeared before the gates of the royal dun.

This time the messenger was Eda. He brought no threats, but an offer to make the plain thick with corn every year without ploughing or sowing.

Fergus was delighted to have his dwarf back again, but still he refused.

'Offer him our treasures, Iubdan,' advised Bebo.

'Listen, Fergus,' said Iubdan to the angry King. 'Isn't it a pity to have Faylinn and Emania tormenting one another? Will you take the best of our magic treasures as ransom? Then we can still be friends.'

'Tell me of your treasures!' said Fergus.

'There is the bronze cauldron with handles of beaten silver. It is beautiful, but the great charm is that no matter how often you empty it that cauldron is always full.'

'What use would a cauldron the size of an acorn be to a man of my hunger?' demanded Fergus. 'I will not have your cauldron.'

'I have a harp,' said Iubdan. 'The sweetest harp in all the world. Yet it needs no harpist. If you are sad, it will play the gayest music. If you are thoughtful, the noblest strains come from it without a finger touching the strings.'

'I like to see the musician,' objected Fergus. 'Half the pleasure is to watch the fingers plucking the strings. You may keep your harp!'

Iubdan told of the needle which sewed without a sewing woman in the room; a spool of thread leagues long, yet so fine it could be shut in the closed hand; a knife that cut without being held; and a pair of water shoes that would fit the smallest or the largest feet and carry the wearer over or under water as easily as on dry land.

'There is a treasure worth having,' advised Eda.

Fergus gave in.

'Give me the water shoes and you can return home.'

Eisirt brought the shoes and, one sunny morning, Bebo and Iubdan

mounted their horse and, with
a mob of singing and cheering
Wee People following them, rode off
home.

They never returned, but ever after
there was friendship between the two
countries. In Faylinn, Eisirt made a long
poem about the giants of Emania and at
the court of Fergus, the favourite story
was of the war with the Wee People.

Midir and Etain

The Bride of the High King

The High King of Ireland, Eochy, had sent a proclamation to all the chiefs and nobles to come to the assembly at Tara.

In a few days messengers began to arrive from every fort and dun. To Eochy's anger not one would come.

'We will not bring our wives and daughters to Tara where there is no Queen to receive them!' came every answer.

Eochy knew they were right, so he sent another proclamation throughout Ireland. He would choose among the noble and beautiful maidens willing to share his throne. He heard of many, but the one he thought most of was Etain, daughter of Etar, and at once he rode out to visit her.

On his way to Etar's dun, Eochy came to a spring where a group of girls had gathered. He checked his horse and from the hilltop looked down on them.

One sat in the middle, combing her hair with a comb of gold and silver. She wore a tunic of green silk and over her shoulders was flung a purple mantle. Her golden hair fell in two long plaits, with golden balls at the end.

Eochy's eyes were keen and he could see her vivid blue eyes, with thin, black eyebrows, and he heard her clear laughter. He had never seen anyone so lovely.

'She must have come from a fairy palace!' he thought. 'If she is willing I'll make her Queen of all Ireland!'

When Etain met the King and saw how much he loved her, she was indeed willing. So she became his wife and Eochy brought her to Tara.

Etain was happy in her new home until there came to the court a wonderful musician and storyteller. No one knew where he came from and no one before had heard the music he played, the songs he sang and the stories he told. They were all about the Land of Youth and, when Etain fell asleep, she dreamed she was there, while the music he had played still sounded in her ears.

One day when they were alone he told her a story.

Long ago, when the people of Dana were driven from Ireland by the Children of Miled, they disappeared into the Land of Youth. Midir the Proud, son of the Dagda, was married to a girl so beautiful there had never been another to equal her and they called her The Fair. Another princess, Fuamnach, became jealous and, by her spells, changed The Fair into a butterfly. When she saw the quivering, pale, yellow wings and knew the loveliness of the girl still lived in the butterfly, Fuamnach raised a violent wind that blew the butterfly out of the palace of Bri Leith.

For seven years The Fair was tossed and driven from one end of Ireland to the other. Her wings were torn and bruised, and she was almost tired of living when one lucky gust hurled her through an archway of Angus's fairy

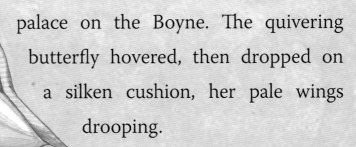

palace on the Boyne. The quivering butterfly hovered, then dropped on a silken cushion, her pale wings drooping.

Angus, who had been watching, stepped near. The Immortals cannot be hidden from one another and he knew the butterfly was an enchanted girl.

'You shall have peace here,' he told her. 'One day we'll find out if there is any way of giving you back your proper form.'

Angus had a sunny bower made, sheltered by flowering bushes and walled with roses. Here The Fair lived, seldom venturing from the palace. Her wings healed and grew larger. After the hardships of those seven years she felt content. Yet she wasn't happy.

Fuamnach heard no more of The Fair and was sure she had driven her away, so that she could never return. Then a stranger spoke of a wonderful butterfly, so rare and lovely, Angus had built a special bower to keep it safe.

'A yellow butterfly with black spots!' thought Fuamnach. 'That is The Fair. I will send her wandering again!'

As the yellow butterfly, at the end of a long sunny day, flew to the bower, a bitter wind swept along the river, caught her up and, tossing her into the air, whirled her over and over.

The Fair flew her swiftest, trying to outdistance the tempest, but she could not. Folding her wings, she let herself be carried along. To her amazement, she saw another palace rising before her. For a moment the wind was held back and she darted into a lofty room, quiet and cool. Had she found her way back to the dun of Angus? wondered The Fair.

Then she saw a man sitting at a long table, eating a ripe apple. Beside him, sat a woman, looking thoughtfully into the drinking cup set before her. As she raised it to her lips the wind rose and the yellow butterfly was flung into the wine. Before she could stop herself, the woman drank the wine, butterfly and all.

By her magic powers, Fuamnach heard the news.

'At last I am rid of The Fair!' she thought.

But not long after, Etar's wife, the woman who had been drinking the wine when the yellow butterfly was blown into the chieftain's palace, had a baby – a little girl with The Fair's eyes and hair. As she grew she had the enchanted girl's ways and loveliness. She was called Etain and grew up without knowing her real origin, though sometimes she had strange dreams and when she awoke, she felt sad and lost.

Midir Explains

'But my name is Etain!' exclaimed the High King's young wife. 'I am the daughter of Etar and you have told me a story about myself!'

'It is a true story!' declared the musician. 'And I am Midir!'

Etain frowned.

'The story is ended!' she told him.

Midir plucked the strings of his harp and played. Etain listened with eyes half-closed. Now he sang:

Etain! In your dreams remember,
Though your waking hours forget.
Here the lonely years have caught you,
Tangled in a magic net.

Strange this land of toil and longing;
Sorrow here is wisdom's truth;
Grey the years and grim the visions;
Golden is the Land of Youth.

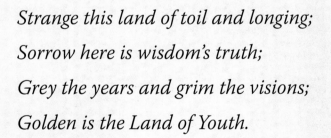

Every day is filled with music;
Every night each moment sings.
Years may pass but time is endless,
Joy's a bird with gleaming wings.

Rise up, Etain! I have sought you
Throughout Erin far and near.
Lay your hand in mine and follow.
Etain! You're a stranger here!

Where the sunset flames the ocean,
Where the moonbeams cross the sea,
Lies the Land of Youth before us.
Fly there, Etain! Fly with me!

Etain was dreaming. The magic of the music carried her into the story Midir had told. She smiled, longing to believe him, yet determined not to.

He drew back from the harp and stood up.

'Etain! Will you come with me to the Land of Youth?'

She shook her head.

'I am wife to the High King of Ireland. Your stories and your songs are delightful. But don't expect me to believe them!'

Midir looked at her sorrowfully. Then he was gone! The strings of the harp quivered as if he had touched them in passing.

A Game of Chess

When the High King returned Etain told him all that had happened. When she repeated Midir's story it became real. She believed it. She sang for the High King the words Midir had sung for her. Then tears came into her eyes and she could not go on.

'It's as well this musician has departed!' declared King Eochy. 'You were wise not to give too much heed to him, Etain.'

That night and many nights following, Etain dreamed she was lost and searching for the way home. When she awoke and found herself in the royal palace at Tara she still felt lost.

Early one summer day, before the gates were open and while Etain still slept, Eochy walked upon the rampart, looking over the wide Plain of Breg.

Without sound or motion a young warrior stood beside him. The stranger wore a purple tunic and his yellow hair reached his shoulders. In one hand he carried a light spear. On his arm was a shield with gems set all round it. His eyes, as he gazed upon the High King, were grey and sparkling, and

Eochy was puzzled, for he knew this man had not been in Tara the night before and he could not have entered that morning.

'I have come to ask your protection,' said the stranger and he saluted the High King.

'I give welcome to the hero who is yet unknown,' replied Eochy. 'Come with me.'

They entered the great hall and went up to the high table.

'I long to play a game of chess with the best player in all Ireland,' the young man told the king.

Eochy loved chess even more than music and singing. He sent for his board of silver marked with precious stones and the carved men in the bag of golden chains, so that they could begin at once.

'What stakes shall we play for?' asked the High King, who knew that few could beat him.

'If I lose I will give you fifty dark grey steeds, eager, spirited, yet so trained they will stop at a touch – or a gift of equal worth,' promised the strange warrior.

Eochy considered this.

'I'd rather have something that will be useful to my people,' he decided. 'If I win, let rocks and stones be cleared from the Plain of Breg, dig out the rushes that make the land barren, build a causeway across yonder bog and cut down that corner of the forest. Do you agree?'

'You shall have that and more – if you win!' promised the stranger.

And he let Eochy win.

The High King knew his opponent was no mortal and he was thankful to have gained so much. But he was cautious.

'What can this stranger really want with me?' he wondered, as they followed the steward to make sure the task was well done.

A host of fairy folk were already at work. Eochy noticed how they harnessed the oxen, with a yoke upon their shoulders instead of a strap over their foreheads. Afterwards he always had it done this way.

Then the High King and the stranger returned to their game. This time the winner was to choose the forfeit.

Now the stranger won.

'I choose a kiss from Etain!' he said.

Eochy sprang to his feet, knocking over the board and the chessmen.

'Who are you?' he demanded.

'I am Midir!' answered the handsome stranger.

'The musician?'

'Midir the Proud, son of the Dagda, Prince of Slieve Callary. Etain was my wife over a thousand years ago. She was exiled from our Land of Youth by a cruel spell and all these years I have searched for her. By chance, coming to your court as a musician, I found her. She will not come with me, so let me have the one kiss!'

Eochy listened without speaking. He loved Etain dearly and he was afraid.

'Return in a month's time!' he said at last. 'Then if Etain is willing, you shall have what you ask.'

Midir's Return

The High King had many worried hours dreading what would happen when Midir came to redeem the promise he had made. He told Etain of the games of chess and she was troubled too. Sometimes the King's Court seemed far away and she entered a country of dreamlike loveliness. As the day for Midir's arrival drew near, she began to dread his coming.

'Yet he can do nothing unless I agree,' she told herself.

Before the day came Eochy had the great hall of Tara surrounded by armed men. As darkness fell and the scullions ran along the walls, lighting the torches, a golden radiance dimmed the glow from the fire and the first flickerings of the torches – and Midir stood before the High King.

Etain, who was pouring wine, let the cup fall and stared at him. She heard music, though the harp stood silent, and voices called her – 'Etain! Etain!'

Midir took her hand in his and, throwing his arm about her, they rose into the air. The roof opened and, for a moment, Eochy saw them hovering.

He rushed from the hall, but all he or the shouting crowd could see was two swans flying towards Slievenamon.

Etain was never again seen at the court of the High King.

The Long Life of Tuan Mac Carrell

One winter morning St Finnan, Abbot of Moville in Donegal, set out from his monastery and walked through the gap in the mountains to the fort of Tuan Mac Carrell. He had never met the chieftain, but he had heard such strange stories about him that he was determined to find out the truth.

The Abbot, in his long robe and sandals, a thick staff in his hand, strode quickly through the settlement which had grown about the gates of the monastery. A rough road led straight through a dark wood, where the trees met overhead and the light was dim. If Finnan glanced right or left he could see stealthy grey shadows creeping from trunk to trunk. But he was too fearless to dread wolves, even by night, while now the sun was showing over the mountain tops and touching the crests of the highest trees.

'Come near me and I'll crack your ugly skulls with a blow of my oak staff!' said the Abbot out loud.

As he came from the shelter of the wood a bitter wind, heavy with snow, swept across the mountains. St Finnan had been walking fast and was hot, but now he shivered and thought he would have been wiser had he waited for a finer day.

'My purpose cannot wait!' he decided. 'Who knows how much time I have left!'

For he hoped to turn the pagan Tuan into a good Christian.

He had not broken his fast and when at last he saw the fort of the Mac Carrells rising before him, Finnan felt so weak his limbs could scarcely carry him.

The outer rampart was built of rocks with a fence of dried thorn bushes on top. A stream of water flowed round and the plank bridge had not yet been thrown over for the gate was still closed. Blue smoke from wood fires rose into the air and Finnan could hear the lowing of cattle and barking of dogs. As he reached the stream the gate opened and a sleepy guard armed with sword and spear looked across at the Abbot.

'Who are you and what do you want?' he demanded.

'I am Finnan, Abbot of Moville, and I have come to preach to Tuan your Chief,' answered the saint.

The man called to another and remained staring curiously at Finnan.

Presently the messenger returned and called to the Abbot: 'Tuan will not allow you to enter. He has no liking for clerics.'

Finnan did not answer. He bent his head, folded his arms and stood at the edge of the stream opposite the gate.

The wind beat in his face and tried to tear away his robe.

Snow piled about his feet and on his shoulders, and flakes were tangled in his hair. Yet he vowed he would not move until Tuan sent for him.

'Then he will cease to be a pagan,' thought Finnan.

Inside the great hall with its blazing fires, Tuan was eating a dish of stewed meat with onions and herbs. As he drained his third horn of mead,

he remembered the Abbot he had refused to see.

'Was the cleric angry when he was forced to return without speaking to me?' he asked.

'The Abbot of Moville is still at the gate!' he was told.

Tuan heard in amazement. Logs burned on the open hearths. The hall was filled with the fragrant smoke. Yet he drew his heavy cloak round his shoulders as the wind howled about the walls.

'The cleric won't wait much longer,' he declared. 'Bring in the hot wine and let us have some music. I hate that screaming wind!'

Tuan tried to forget Finnan. But as the long winter night came on and lighted torches were fixed against the walls, he asked: 'Which way did the Abbot go? There are wolves in the forest these dark, cold nights.'

'Finnan of Moville is still at your gate!' was the answer.

Then Tuan sprang to his feet, marched down the hall, out across the lios or enclosure, to the gate. At the far side of the stream stood Finnan, a white statue, without moving.

'Put over the bridge!' ordered Tuan.

When that was done he ran across and seized the Abbot's arm.

'Forgive me!' he said. 'I have broken the laws of hospitality. I have behaved not like a Chief but a scullion. You shall say whatever you choose within my fort.'

He brushed away the snow and putting his arm about Finnan, helped him over the bridge and into the hall.

'Ask what you please,' he said. 'Everything I have is yours!'

'Let me preach to you and your people, or I will go back and stand once more before your gate!' was Finnan's answer.

'You shall preach to us as long as you wish,' promised Tuan.

The Abbot sat in the chieftain's chair and spoke to him and to all those who could crowd into the hall. Before the winter was over there wasn't a pagan left within the dun of Mac Carrells. They were all Christians, while Tuan and Finnan had become great friends. The monks came and went, and Tuan's people were always welcome at Moville.

On a spring day Tuan and the Abbot sat before the door of the great hall talking.

'I have heard that you have lived a very long time, Tuan,' said Finnan. 'But you look a young man.'

'I am a young man,' Tuan told him. 'Yet I have lived longer than any other man and not always as a man. Listen now!'

Finnan listened.

'You know me as Tuan, son of Carrell,' said the chief. 'But once I was son of Starn, and he was brother to Partholan, the first man who ever settled in Ireland.'

'Was the land empty?' asked Finnan.

'There were no human beings here,' replied Tuan. 'But a race of demons, Fomorians, cruel and ugly, ranged over the country. Partholan could not make peace with them. Whatever he tried to do they destroyed. So he made war against them, fighting battle after battle and giving the Fomorians no rest until they fled in their boats to the Northern Seas.'

'I have heard of Fomorian giants,' and Finnan. 'The women in the settlement sing songs about them to frighten bold children.'

'They wouldn't be singing songs about them if we hadn't driven the whole misshapen race away!' exclaimed the Chief. 'When they were gone we had peace. Partholan was a great builder and as protection from the Fomorians he taught us to make strong fortresses. We built roads and bridges over the nine rivers and we had boats on the three lakes.'

'You couldn't count the rivers and lakes in Ireland now. Has the country changed?' asked Finnan.

'Indeed it has!' Tuan told him. 'I saw the rivers increase as the people grew in numbers. Then a terrible sickness came upon us. Those who lay down to sleep never stood up again. Men dropped as they walked upon the roads. Children died as they played and women fell lifeless over their spinning wheels. When Partholan died I was the only man in the land, for there is always one left to tell the story.

'At first I could not believe that all the men and women I knew were gone. I journeyed from fort to fort to find each more silent and desolate. There were stores of grain and dried meat – food for a nation – so I did not go hungry. When my clothes wore out I found plenty more, woven and stitched for the dead Partholanians. At first I talked to myself for the comfort of hearing a human voice. Then it frightened me and I became silent. For twenty years I suffered the most terrible loneliness ever heard of. I almost envied the wolves, which increased until enormous packs roamed the forests.

'Then I grew old and feeble. I gathered stores into a cave halfway up a cliff. It was dry and safe, and seemed less lonely than the forts, for no one else had lived there and there was nothing to remind me that my race had passed away.

'The sun shone right into the entrance of the cave. I lay half asleep, stretched on the warm rock and looking down upon the shore, deserted except for a flock of long-legged seabirds which waded along the edge hunting for food.

'While I watched a boat came slowly into sight. A tattered rag fastened to an oar lashed upright was the only sail and I could see the occupants busy bailing out the water. As it was beached a tall, haggard man leaped out and gazed about him. Even at the distance and after so many years I knew him.

'He was Nemed, son of Agnoman, my father's brother!

'Instead of rushing down, welcoming him, telling what had happened to Partholan and all his people and so ending my loneliness, I had grown so savage and accustomed to my solitary life, I hid behind a rock and watched the newcomers unloading until the sun set.

'There were only nine people in that boat, four men and four women, as well as Nemed. Afterwards I learned that when they set out on their expedition there were thirty-two boats, with thirty men and women in each. Storms had driven them from their course, the stars were hidden, food and water were exhausted and only one of the boats with these few worn-out survivors reached Ireland.

'I slept well that night and when I awoke, saw the smoke from a fire of logs, and those nine people gathered round it.

'I stood up to go down to them. I no longer felt old and wretched, but I knew some great change had come upon me. On my head were two branching horns, my feet were hoofs, my skin had turned to hide. I was no longer a man, but a stag!'

'A stag!' exclaimed Finnan.

'I bounded from the cave,' continued Tuan. 'I was young and strong once more and while Nemed and his crew were fighting against the Fomorians who returned to Ireland, I went through the forests, over the mountains, gathering the deer into a great herd. I saw the Nemedians build new homes, for they were afraid of the empty, ruined forts of the Partholanians. Their numbers increased and often the sound of their horns woke me from confused dreams.'

'You were hunted?' asked Finnan, pityingly.

Tuan smiled.

'I was hunted, but not one came within sight of the King of the Stags. Often I was near them, for I remembered the days when I was a hunter and a singer of songs. From overhanging rocks or clumps of trees, I saw the Nemedians, my own people. There were times when I longed to draw nearer and cry out to them. But I knew before they could hear my words, their dogs would be upon me and their spears would take my life.'

Tuan sat silent.

'And then?' murmured the Abbot.

'My spreading antlers were growing to an incredible size. They pressed upon my head, and my legs, so swift and slender, stumbled under the burden. They became entangled in trees and once the whole herd waited while I wrestled with a flowering creeper which clung about me. As I dragged myself free, a young stag stamped upon the ground and challenged me. When he flung back his head and bellowed his defiance, I realised that it was age which bent my neck and sent me stumbling where once I had trod securely.

'Our horns entwined, we pulled and thrust and, when the combat was ended, I remained King. After the third challenge, though victorious, I was weary of stagdom. At night I left the herd. Slowly I returned to the cave and stood in the moonlight, longing for the sun to rise, longing to be a man again, yet wondering if I would wake the next day!'

'What happened?' demanded Finnan impatiently.

'I slept. I awoke. My antlers lay upon the ledge before the cave. My slender legs had become short, my head was long and sharp tusks projected from my mouth. I had changed to a boar.

'Young and fierce I rushed headlong to the plain. It was deserted. The homes of the Nemedians lay empty and silent. I had seen, without noticing, the strange disease which had destroyed the Partholanians sweep through the newer settlements. Not one was left alive, to hunt or be hunted.

'Angrily I raged through the forests, feeding on beech mast, fighting other boars, leading a trotting, grunting herd I detested.

'I remembered I had been King of the Stags of Ireland – proud, swift, handsome! I remembered when I was one of Partholan's warriors, one of his council, brave and learned. Now I was a boar and I determined to be King of the Boars!

'And so it was, though I knew no happiness in my swinish subjects.

'I was almost glad when my youth left me. I felt sure that in my next life I would be a man. I made up my mind to go in search of other human beings, bring them to Ireland and re-people the deserted settlements, build bridges, make roads.

'Gladly I stretched myself at the back of the magic cave and grunted with joy as I thought that never again would I feed on the rough, tasteless mast, or go trotting and grunting, leader of hundreds of pigs.

'My dreams were happy. The sun roused me and I discovered myself perched upon the summit of a rock outside the cave. I was an eagle, a golden eagle, and my glorious wings glittered in the spreading light. With a scream of delight I sprang into the air and soared up, up, up, up – to greet the sun!

'The cave became my home and, flying above the treetops, I learned to know my own country.

'I saw the Firbolgs land in their leather boats and wondered at their strong, ugly weapons. They lived among the rocks where giant trees had fallen and, in falling, made rough shelters.

'When they began to build, they used the largest stones they could find and made forts strong and ugly as themselves.

'One day I flew above the clouds for I had grown tired of looking upon the Firbolgs where once the Nemedians and the Partholanians had lived. Suddenly I heard singing and music so lovely I remained hovering, wings outspread, until the clouds parted and I saw four magical cities where there had been none before. My eyes had grown used to the gloomy dwellings of the Firbolgs, the empty forts of Nemedians and Partholanians. Now I looked upon shining domes and turrets surrounded by gardens. Glittering walls rose between and bronze gates of intricate design guarded the entrances. Fountains flung their spray high as the tallest trees and the people who lived there were graceful and good to look upon.

'The people of Dana had descended upon Ireland and these were the cities of Falias, Gorias, Finias and Murias. In each city the chief was a wise man who taught poetry, science, craftsmanship and the game of chess. Each city possessed one of their treasures. In Falias was kept the Lia Fail, or Stone of Destiny, on which in after years the High Kings of Ireland stood while they were being crowned. Gorias guarded the invincible sword of Lugh of the Long Arm. In Finias lay a magic spear and Murias had charge of the Cauldron of the Dagda, the Cauldron of Plenty which could feed a host without being emptied.

'I saw the coming of the Milesians and the downfall of the Danaans. I flew overhead when Amergin, son of Miled, stepped on shore. He was the first poet of Ireland and his chant came up to me:

I am the wind that blows over the ocean;
I am the wave of the sea;

I am the ox and a ray of the sun,

The vulture and all that can be;

I am the fairest, the rarest of flowers,

The salmon that swims in the lake,

And I am the thought in the poet's mind,

The craft of the man who can make.

I know of the stars, the moon and the sun.

I am the spear and the battle won.

'I grieved when the wonder and beauty of the Danaans became hidden. They are still in Ireland but only the gifted few can see or hear them.'

Tuan's head sunk on his chest. There was sorrow in his face.

'And then?' whispered Finnan.

The pagan chief lifted his head and smiled proudly.

'When next I changed my shape I was a salmon, though not, my grief, the Salmon of Wisdom. Down to the sea I sped and cut through the waves like a sword. I roamed the oceans of the world, yet back I came to the river I knew. One day I was caught by a fisherman in a net too strong for me to break. I was brought to the wife of Carrell, a chieftain. I was slain and cooked, and she ate the whole of me – bones, skin and all! When I woke again I was Tuan son of Carrell.'

'This should be written in a book of wonders for future generations to read!' declared the Abbot.

The Voyage of Maeldun

One morning in the graveyard at Doocloone, Maeldun, a young man who belonged to the Owens of Aran, was competing with a few friends in putting the stone. They were using the great blocks from the ruined church. The blocks were so heavy that Maeldun was winning easily for, though he was careless and easy-going, he was so strong that not one of his companions could beat him.

Among the crowd, who watched, was a young man who had fallen out of the game right at the start. He hated Maeldun, who was so good at running he could race a swift horse and was able to throw a ball so far there was little chance of finding it again.

He scowled angrily as Maeldun lifted a huge stone to his shoulder and flung it easily, laughing with pleasure at his own strength.

'Isn't it a pity you haven't something better to do than cast stones at Doocloone!' he jeered.

Maeldun turned to him in amazement.

'What could be better than casting stones on a clear, cold morning and the wind blowing from the sea?' he asked.

'If my father had been killed here and the church burned over him, I wouldn't be playing over his grave!' declared the other.

Maeldun no longer smiled. He walked over the rough and blackened ground until he stood in front of his enemy.

'You say my father was killed here!' he said.

'You seem to be the only one that doesn't know it,' muttered the young man bitterly.

'Can you tell me who killed him?' asked Maeldun quietly.

The other drew back. He was sorry he had spoken. But Maeldun was gazing at him sternly, waiting.

'Raiders from Leix,' came the answer. 'They slew him on that spot where you were standing and burned the church over him.'

Maeldun went slowly away, very different from the gay young man who had set out that morning. He told his mother all he had heard.

'It is true!' she said sadly. 'I didn't tell you how Ailell, your father, died, for it spoiled my life and I didn't want it to spoil yours.'

'He must be avenged!' declared Maeldun. 'I'll seek out his murderers if I have to go to the end of the world to find them. How can I get to Leix?'

'Only by sea!'

Maeldun had no boat, so he decided to build a coracle. His two friends – German and Diurnan the Rhymer – went with him to the island Druid for advice.

The Druid listened to the story in silence.

'Sometimes forgiveness is better than vengeance,' he said. 'But if you must seek your father's enemy, make your coracle with three thicknesses of skin. Take only seventeen men with you. Begin building the boat on the first day of the new moon.'

All the young men in the island who hoped to share in the expedition, offered to help. But Maeldun picked out the seventeen he wanted and would not allow any others to touch the boat.

At last it was launched, their stores taken on board and as shouts of farewell came from their friends and families' they hoisted the sail.

As the wind caught it, Maeldun's three young foster brothers came running down the beach calling him to take them.

'Go home!' shouted Maeldun. 'You know I'm forbidden to take more than seventeen. Go home!'

But the boys jumped into the sea and swam after the boat. The waves were so rough they were being swept away when German pulled the smallest on board. Diurnan caught hold of another, while the third clambered in at the stern.

'It can make no difference,' muttered Maeldun. 'And I could not leave them to drown.'

When the wind dropped, the young men took turns at rowing. During the night, to give the rowers a rest, Maeldun once more put up the sail, though there was little wind. When morning came, they were near a small rocky island with a round fort standing in the middle. Spears came whizzing through the air from over the wall and a voice cried: 'I am the better man, for I killed Ailell of the Edge-of-Battle and burned the church of Doocloone

over his body. Yet not one of his kinsmen has tried to find me and avenge his death. You have never done such a deed!'

'I never dreamt of finding my father's murderer in such a place!' exclaimed Maeldun.

'Our journey is over before we're properly started,' grumbled German, feeling quite disappointed.

'God has guided us!' said Diurnan the Rhymer.

Maeldun steered the boat in and, in spite of the shower of spears, which continued to fall about them, was about to leap on shore when a sudden

squall swept them away from the island and all night long rain and wind beat on them until they had no notion where they could be.

'This is your fault!' exclaimed Maeldun to his foster brothers. 'You knew the Druid had warned me, I must take only seventeen. This may be the beginning of our misfortunes!'

The boys looked so unhappy, Maeldun was ashamed of his anger.

'If they hadn't been so young, I might have chosen them myself,' he thought.

They drifted where wind and tide carried them, for Maeldun could not tell whether to go north or south, but hoped they might reach land where the inhabitants would direct them.

The third morning they heard the sound of waves beating against rocks and, as the sun rose, saw a flat, stony island. They were about to row in when a swarm of huge ants came scuttling along the beach. They looked so ferocious that Maeldun turned the boat round and they had to row their hardest, for the ants plunged into the sea and swam after them.

The voyagers came to many islands. There was one with built-up terraces and groves of trees with monstrous birds sitting in the branches. German and Diurnan landed on a flat island where they found an enormous racecourse. They heard shouts and saw gigantic white and brown horses running along the course, but they could see no people.

Diurnan the Rhymer sang of them:

Strange seas, strange islands
Strange as dreams.
I wonder if my eyes are closed.
If still earth's sunlight gleams.

Even Maeldun and his two friends were growing tired of the boat. They all longed for land where they could rest and stretch their limbs. The meat and meal they had brought with them was eaten and all they had was the fish they caught and rain water. When land, with trees growing to the edge of the shore, each loaded with golden apples, rose from the waves, they

cheered with delight. As the boat drew nearer, they saw red swine running among the trees and kicking the trunks until the apples fell on the grass. Then they gorged themselves.

Maeldun and his companions gathered all the apples they had room for and, until they had eaten the last one, they needed no other food or drink.

But when the golden apples were finished, then indeed they knew hunger and thirst. The younger ones longed for home and doubted if they would ever see it again. Maeldun was listening to their complaints when he saw an island with a tall, white tower rising from the centre. A great rampart was built about it and on each side were houses, white as if made of chalk.

Hiding the coracle behind some rocks, the men landed and went into the tower. They found a lofty hall with four low stone pillars in the middle and a great curving staircase at the end. There were no people, only a little black cat which was leaping from pillar to pillar. It looked at the Irish travellers but did not stop. On the walls hung rows of brooches, torcs of gold and silver, swords with gold and silver hilts and jewelled necklaces.

But what Maeldun liked better than all the treasures, was a table laid for a feast with roast meat and tall cups of wine. 'Was this left for us?' Maeldun asked the little cat.

It stopped to listen to him, then went on jumping. They sat down at the table and ate and drank until they were satisfied. Afterwards they lay on wide, cushioned seats which were all along one side of the hall, covered themselves with heavy silk quilts and slept as they had not slept since leaving Aran. Next day they took what was left of the food, but Maeldun wouldn't

allow his companions to touch the brooches or swords, or the silken quilts and garments which lay on the seats.

As they were going out of the door, the youngest of Maeldun's foster brothers ran back and snatched an emerald necklace from its hook.

With a furious snarl, the black cat leaped at him and he fell in a heap of ashes on the floor.

Maeldun put the necklace back in its place, picked up the angry little creature and smoothed its fur. When they went out, the cat was once more jumping from pillar to pillar.

They began to lose count of time. Maeldun thought the young moon had appeared to them seven times. German was sure it must be twice as many. Diurnan couldn't remember at all.

They still had a little dry bread and, when that was eaten they kept the nets out the whole time.

Diurnan told stories and sang to keep his companions from thinking of their hardships.

'We should turn back,' said one. 'There were other houses on the island where the little black cat lived. This sea seems empty of fish, but we might find more food and drink. Isn't it foolish to wander all our lives! I could be happy there!'

'Do you remember what happened to

my brother?' asked the second foster brother. 'I would not go back to that island for all the food in the world.'

While they talked the Rhymer was singing softly:

I longed to sail far where the sky
Bends down and earth's great ocean ends.
But now I long for little roads,
For soft blue smoke, for home and friends.

German and Maeldun watched. As the sun went down, a swift tide carried them into a harbour. Maeldun and the Rhymer climbed from the boat by narrow steps set in the harbour wall and saw before them a huge mill. A wide road led up to it and men hurried by, bent with the weight of heavy sacks.

There was no door but an open archway and the two strangers followed the men with the sacks into a vast chamber almost filled with a millstone.

In the dim light they saw a giant miller grinding away. The men emptied their sacks in a chamber at one side and filled them at the opposite end, where grey, coarse flour fell in a heap.

The miller grinned at them. But there was no friendliness in his eyes.

'You have a right to see the work we do here,' he said. 'For half the corn of your country is ground in this mill. In those sacks is brought all that men grudge one another. You can carry away all you want. But take my advice and do not touch the corn we grind.'

'This is an evil task,' said Diurnan to Maeldun.

So they crossed themselves and went back to their comrades.

Once more they had nothing to eat but the fish which came into their nets. They dried it in the sun. But only Maeldun, the Rhymer and German could eat it without grumbling. The men were sighing and groaning when they came to an island of black people, who wept and lamented all day, though there seemed no reason for their sorrow. Maeldun's second foster brother insisted on going ashore to learn what caused their misery. He, too, turned black and began weeping like the rest.

Maeldun sent two more to bring him back, but they also became black and began to weep. Four others went after them, but they wrapped their

heads in their cloaks, so that they would not breathe the air of the island.

They managed to seize the two men but not the young foster brother and the boat had to sail without him. The two who were rescued couldn't explain what had happened to them. They saw others weeping so they wept. As the island faded into the distance, their own colour returned to them and they ceased weeping.

Many islands were scattered over that ocean and Diurnan declared that if they lived to be very old men, they would have tales to tell throughout the dark winter nights, yet need never tell the same story twice.

One island had a high fortress, frowning over the sea, with a bronze door in the centre. Leaving a guard on the ship, the others landed and came to a glass bridge, with bronze parapets crossing a wide moat which surrounded the fortress.

Keeping together, they stepped on the bridge but it flung them back. As they scrambled up, a woman came out of the fortress with a bucket in her hand. They shouted, but, without looking at them, she let down the bucket, drew water from the moat and returned to the fortress. Determined to enter, Maeldun struck the side of the bridge. The metal quivered and soft music came from it. His eyes closed. He slipped to the ground, asleep, and his companions lay sleeping beside him. The next day when they woke, the woman was coming out of the fortress with her bucket. She laughed at their foolishness, but they would not go away.

Three days they tried to cross the bridge and each time they failed.

On the fourth day, when the woman came out on the bridge, she no longer carried a bucket, but was dressed in white silk with a golden circlet on her long fair hair and silver sandals on her feet.

She came right across the bridge and this time her smile was friendly.

'You are welcome, Maeldun, and you, Rhymer, and German, and every man of your crew. Come with me!'

They marched behind her over the glass bridge. The bronze gate of the fortress stood wide open and they went in with her. She put them at a table arranged with plates and goblets, but they were all empty. She filled them from her bucket, giving each man what he liked best, of food and wine.

They lay on couches and their dreams were the happiest they had known. Yet when they woke they were crowded in their boat, the sail swelled in the wind and there was no trace on the sea of the island, the fortress, or the woman with the bucket.

'I never heard of these islands before,' said Diurnan the Rhymer. 'Strange that of all the ones that sailed from our country, none came this way.'

'Maybe they came, but could not return,' Maeldun told him. 'If we keep on, we shall come to the edge of the world.'

The wind had fallen and for days they took turns at the oars. Diurnan sang and recited poems which made them forget danger and loneliness, and kept their minds on the wonder of their wanderings.

He was silent when they saw a great square silver column rising up from the water. It towered into the sky so that they could not see the top. A silver net spread from it, so large they sailed through the mesh. Diurnan drew his sword and hacked off a piece.

'Do not destroy this work of mighty men!'
Maeldun warned him.

'I want our tale to be believed when we return
home,' replied the Rhymer. 'If ever we reach Ireland
again, I will lay this piece of silver on the High Altar
of Armagh in honour of God's name.'

A voice cried out from the top of the pillar –
clear like a clarion. But they could not understand
the words it spoke.

I saw a web float o'er the sea,
A silver web dropped from the skies.
I heard a voice that caught my soul,
So loud, serene and wise.

murmured Diurnan to himself as they sailed
on, marvelling.

A mist hid the silver column from them. But an island loomed up and, stepping from the boat, they waded to the beach, dragging the boat after them.

A wall rose before them. Walking round it to find an entrance, they came to a grassy mound and, climbing to the top, found themselves in sunshine. They sat there looking over the wall, which enclosed a mansion. At one side a marble bath sunk in the ground was being filled with water by seventeen girls. The clatter of a horse's hoofs sounded from the other side and a grandly dressed woman rode up to the house. She jumped down and a girl took the horse. Presently the rider went into the bath. A girl came through an unseen gateway in the wall and called to Maeldun and his men. 'The Queen invites you,' she said.

Gladly they obeyed, went down from the mound, in through the doorway they had not seen and up to the house. There a feast was ready. Maeldun sat opposite the Queen and each of his crew sat with one of the girls. At night they were given good beds and, when morning came, they were so refreshed all their troubles were forgotten. But, when they prepared to go, the Queen stopped them.

'Stay here,' she said. 'You will never find your home again, so where is the sense in wandering from island to island, only to perish miserably at the end? Stay here! You do not know the wonders of this island. There is no age or sickness here and there is room for all of you.'

Maeldun looked at his crew who had suffered so greatly.

'Shall we stay?' he asked.

'We will!' shouted each one of them.

The Queen told Maeldun that her husband had been King of the island and the seventeen girls were their daughters. Now the King was dead and she ruled. There were many other people on the island and all day she went among them, but came back at night.

Maeldun was happy there. So were they all for three months. But the crew soon forgot their hardships and began to long for their own country. It seemed to them that they had been away for years and they implored him to sail on.

'Where would we have a better life than we have here?' asked Maeldun. 'Let us stay a while.'

Even Diurnan and German were tired of the island and they told him that, if he wished to stay, they would go without him. But Maeldun could not bear to part with his friends and, to please him, they stayed, though they grumbled all the time.

One day Diurnan and German decided to take the boat and depart at once. Maeldun declared he had changed his mind and would go with them.

The Queen was away trying to settle a quarrel among some of her people. They loaded the boat with provisions, put out the oars and pushed off. The Queen, riding home, saw their sail as it caught the wind. She had a ball of cord in her hand and, holding one end, flung the ball after them. Maeldun caught the ball and she drew them back.

Maeldun had been sorry to leave the island without saying goodbye, but now he was as determined as the others to depart. The next time the

Queen was away from the fort, they boarded the boat again. They were scarcely an oar's length from the shore when she came riding up. Once more she flung the ball of string. Once more Maeldun caught it and they were drawn back.

Again this happened and the crew looked strangely at Maeldun.

'Why do you hold the ball?' asked German. 'If you would sooner stay, why pretend? We can sail the boat without you!'

'Indeed I don't hold it. The ball clings to my hand,' protested Maeldun. 'I am honest with you. I have been very happy here, but I long for home.'

So the next time, one of the crew caught the ball and when he could not let go, Diurnan cut off his hand and it fell into the sea. Away sped the boat. But the Queen on her horse wept, so that tears poured down her face and the seventeen girls wept with her, while from all over the island rose cries of sorrow.

Maeldun, with tears in his eyes, looked backward, as long as he could see the island where he had been treated as a King.

There was no wind and the soft air made them lazy so that the oars barely feathered the heaving sea. Yet the boat moved swiftly in a current which carried them round an island thickly wooded on one half and with a wide stretch of grassland covering the other. Sheep grazed beside a lake and when the current brought them into a curved bay, they found an ancient fort and a small church where an old monk was saying Mass.

'Who are you, holy man?' asked Maeldun, when they came out into the sunshine once more.

'I am one of the monks who went on an ocean pilgrimage with St Brendan of Birr,' said the monk. 'And I am the only one left alive.'

The old man had so much to tell them and was so pleased with their company that they stayed with him while they cleaned the boat, mended the sail and collected food.

One day Maeldun saw a dark cloud, driving from the south-west. It came so quickly he guessed it could not be a real cloud and as it drew near, he saw that it was a great eagle with faltering wings, carrying a red-berried branch

in its talons. It dropped beside the lake and began eating the berries, big as grapes. Some of the juice and skins fell into the lake until the water looked like wine.

Diurnan and German coming in search of Mael-dun, hid with him among the trees and watched the great bird, fearing that if they showed themselves, it would seize them in its curved claws and carry them off, though it seemed old and sick, and its dull plumage was thin. But when Maeldun walked down to the lake, the bird took no notice and presently the others followed him. They gathered some of the fallen berries and still the eagle did not look at them.

As they walked away, two smaller eagles flew down and began cleaning and smoothing the old bird's feathers. The next day the birds were still there, and the day after the big eagle plunged into the lake. When it came out the watchers saw that its plumage was clean and glossy, old age had gone from it and it was a young, strong eagle who flew away out of sight, its helpers trying to keep up with it.

'Let us become young like the eagle,' suggested Diurnan. 'I am old from hardship and travelling.'

'No! No!' cried Maeldun. 'The bird may have poisoned the water.'

But Diurnan slipped in, swam in the lake and drank the crimson water. From that day he was never tired or sick. His eyes were always clear and keen, his teeth strong and, to the last hour of his long life, he was like a young man.

They said goodbye to the old monk of Birr and sailed on.

Diurnan was singing about the eagle when they heard loud laughter and shouts of enjoyment. Towards dawn they reached an island where they could see men and women dancing, tossing balls to one another and laughing all the time.

'There's no sense in landing here,' said Maeldun.

But as several men longed to know what made the islanders so merry he let them draw lots for the one who should go on shore. His own foster

brother, the last of the three, was winner. The moment he set foot on the island, he began to laugh and jig about like the others. Maeldun shouted to him to come back, but he would not and, in the end, they left him there, still laughing and dancing.

Maeldun's three brothers were gone from the ship, one dead, one on the island of the black mourners and now, the last of them left behind with the laughing people.

'Maybe our voyage is coming to an end,' said Maeldun. 'I am tired of strange places, yet how can I return without avenging my father!'

Just then they saw a white patch floating on the water.

They thought it a wounded seabird, but when they came up with it, they found an old, old man, covered in his long white hair and beard which grew to his feet. He lay on a broad, flat rock without shelter.

'Come with us in the boat!' urged Maeldun, who was sorry for the man's desolation. 'How have you come to such misery?'

'Do not grieve for me,' the old man told them. 'Listen, now! I belonged to Tory Island. I was born and grew up there. Have you heard of the monastery of Tory? I was the cook. All around me were good, holy men. Yet daily I took the food and sold it to passing ships for grand clothes and golden ornaments and even manuscripts bound in jewelled leather. Because I wasn't found out I grew proud and thought myself the cleverest man on Tory.

'One day I filled a boat with all my treasures and started away so that I could live grandly where no one knew I had been a cook. A storm came up

and I was terrified. But, when the wind dropped, the boat lay becalmed and there before me was an angel standing on the water.

'"Where are you going?" he asked.

'"To lead a comfortable, pleasant life for the rest of my days," I told him.

'"You would not think it pleasant if you could see the demons gathered round you. Because of your greed and pride, the boat will not move and unless you do as I tell you, your road will take you straight to hell."

'I was frightened and began to feel sorry as well.

'"Tell me what to do?" I said.

'"Throw all you have stolen into the sea," commanded the angel. "And where the boat brings you, there you must stay."

'I threw out my beautiful clothes, the jewelled books and gleaming ornaments, until all I had left was a little wooden cup which really was my own. The boat brought me to this bare rock and here I have been for seven years. Otters bring me salmon from the sea and every day this cup is filled with good wine. I have all eternity to think about and I never feel cold or wet.'

Then Maeldun told his story.

'You will find the man who killed your father, Maeldun,' said the cook. 'But don't kill him. What good would it do your father? God has saved you from great dangers. And have you never done wrong? Forgive your enemy, then you will go back to your own country in peace.'

Maeldun thanked him and they went on.

As darkness came they reached a small island.

'We have seen this before,' said Maeldun.

It was the island where the murderer of his father lived.

The coracle grated gently on the strand. They lifted it up and went quietly to the fort. The gate was open. The door of the hall where the company sat at their evening meal was open and there were no men on guard.

'What would you do if you saw Maeldun?' asked one.

'I would give him a great welcome!' declared the chief man, the slayer of Ailell. 'For if he lives he has had great toil and suffering through my evil doing, and I would ask him to forgive me.'

Maeldun beat on the door with his spear.

'Who is there?' cried the Chief.

'Maeldun is here!' he answered.

They entered in peace and were given such a welcome it made the whole voyage seem worthwhile. Diurnan the Rhymer told the story of the wanderings. The night went on and another day had come before that story was ended.

They went home easily and in comfort. But the Rhymer journeyed on to Armagh and laid upon the High Altar the piece of wrought silver he had hewn from the silver net.

There he again told the story of the Voyage of Maeldun.

Glossary

Caman	A hurley
Coracle	A small, light boat made from woven rods and animal skins, similar to, but smaller than, a curragh
Creel	A type of small wicker basket
Curragh	A small boat of wood and canvas
Dagda	The leader of the ancient Irish gods
Diadem	A type of crown
Druids	Learned wise men, often believed to be magicians, who worshipped pagan gods
Dun	A fort
Firbolg	Rulers of Ireland before the Tuatha de Danaan
Fomorians	A semi-divine mythical race who lived in Ireland before the arrival of the Celts, at the same time as the Tuatha de Danaan
Geis	A solemn instruction, especially of a magical kind, the violation of which led to misfortune or even death
Grianan	A sunroom
Lugh (or Lug)	An ancient Irish god, often represented as a sun god
Putting the stone	Throwing a stone/rock
Rath	A ring-fort
Scullion	A kitchen boy who helps the cook, washes dishes etc.
Tuatha de Danaan	A semi-divine mythical race who lived in Ireland before the arrival of the Celts
Ultonian	An Ulsterman

About the Author

PATRICIA LYNCH was born in Cork in 1898 and educated in Ireland, England and Belgium. Though only eighteen at the time, she reported on the events of the 1916 rising in Dublin for *The Suffragette* and Sylvia Pankhurst's newspaper *The Workers' Dreadnought*. She married writer Richard Michael Fox in 1922 and in the following years began to build her career as a writer. She had an incredibly prolific writing career, writing some fifty novels and 200 short stories. *The Turf-Cutter's Donkey* series featured drawings by Jack B. Yeats and is perhaps her best-known series, although the well-received Brogeen series would come a close second.

Lynch's writing was rich with the enchantment and magic of Irish history and culture. She also wrote a more autobiographical work, *A Storyteller's Childhood*. Following the death of her husband in 1969 she moved into the home of her close friends Eugene and Mai Lambert of Lambert Puppet Theatre fame. She died in 1972.

About the Illustrator

SARA BAKER won the Mercier Illustrators' Competition organised by Mercier Press to find an original talent to illustrate this new edition of Patricia Lynch's stories. Sara is originally from Northern Ireland and developed a love of drawing at a very young age. She studied and lived in England for many years. In 2004 she moved to Baltimore, West Cork with her husband and two daughters ... for an adventure. She was told about the competition by a friend and decided to investigate further. 'While I was reading [the Kingdom of the Dwarfs] I just knew I would enter, as the pictures were coming thick and fast in my imagination.' On winning the competition she created a series of stunning watercolour illustrations for these stories which will enchant and delight a new generation of readers of all ages.